Triplets

Annabel's Perfect Party

HOLLY WEBB

SCHOLASTIC

Scholastic Children's Books
An imprint of Scholastic Ltd
Euston House, 24 Eversholt Street
London, NW1 1DB, UK
Registered office: Westfield Road, Southam, Warwickshire, CV47 0RA
SCHOLASTIC and associated logos are trademarks and/or registered trademarks of
Scholastic Inc.

First published in the UK by Scholastic Ltd, 2004
This edition published by Scholastic Ltd, 2014

ISBN 978 1407 14475 7

British Library Cataloguing-in-Publication Data.
A CIP catalogue record for this book is available from the British Library.

Printed by CPI Group (UK) Ltd, Croydon, CR0 4YY
Papers used by Scholastic Children's Books are made from wood grown in
sustainable forests.

1 3 5 7 9 10 8 6 4 2

www.scholastic.co.uk

Chapter One

It was Monday lunchtime at Manor Hill School. The dining hall was full to bursting and *really* noisy. Mrs Andrews, the teacher on duty, had already had a go at shushing everybody, but now she'd more or less given up. After a weekend when they could talk as much as they wanted, and then a morning in school where they were supposed to be practically silent, lunchtime was a chance to chat – and everyone was making the most of it.

The Ryan triplets had bagged one of the choice tables in the corner by the windows. It had a good view of anything that might be going on in the rest of the dining hall, and the

1

playground. And it was as far away from Mrs Andrews as possible. They'd had to make a dash for it right under the noses of some very snotty Year Eight girls, and there'd been some serious muttering along the lines of "How dare they?" and "Little *brats*!" But they didn't care. (Well, Becky did, but she'd just stared very hard at the kitten on her lunchbox and pretended not to hear.) Katie and Annabel had no such qualms, and gazed back at the Year Eights, Annabel with a sunny "So what?" smile, while Katie folded her arms and cheekily dared them to make her move.

"Coward!" teased Annabel cheerfully, as she banged her lunchbox down next to Becky, and flounced on to a chair. Katie gave the Year Eights one last warning glare and sat down too. "Yeah, Becky, honestly – what did you think they were going to do to us?"

Becky flushed scarlet. "It's not fair – you two are so good at arguing! I'm brilliant at it too – half an hour after whoever it is has left

I've got the best comebacks. It's just that at the time I can't think of anything to say."

"Never mind," comforted Annabel. "You've got us to stick up for you."

Becky sighed. It was true, but sometimes she wished she could manage without her sisters – if she really had to.

Saima, Megan and Fran came up with their lunch trays, loaded with grim-looking school dinners.

"Excellent," said Saima happily, "I thought Marie and her lot were going to make you move."

The triplets grinned to each other as their friends set down their trays. Then Annabel made a face. "Fran, what *is* that?" she complained, pointing at the plate of something-and-chips on Fran's tray.

"Well . . . chips."

"And?"

"I don't know," Fran admitted sadly. "I was kind of dithering and the Haggis just dumped it on my plate. It *could* be shepherd's pie. That was on the menu, anyway." Everybody looked over at the counter and giggled. They could see why Fran hadn't argued. Mrs Hagan, aka the Haggis, was the head dinner lady, and she was really fierce.

"*I* know what that is," said a voice over Fran's shoulder. It was Jack, a boy from their class, on his way to the next table. "It's haggis – Mrs Hagan's speciality. You know what haggis actually is, don't you?" he added, grinning at the girls.

"No," sighed Fran, "but I have a feeling you're going to tell me. Go on."

"Weeelll . . . basically, it's bits. Bits of sheep. But the really *special* thing. . ." Jack paused, enjoying the moment. "The *best* bit, is that it's all wrapped up in a sheep's *stomach*. And that's what that is." He beamed at Fran, who looked down at her dinner in dismay.

"Ohh. Are you hungry, Jack?" she asked hopefully, as everyone groaned and made sick noises.

"No. Way." He chortled. "You're not getting rid of it that easily. Just eat the chips from round the edges, and try not to get any of the stomachy bits. . ." Then he went to sit down, still giggling.

"He is such a liar," said Becky reassuringly. "I'm sure it's shepherd's pie, Fran, honestly. Jack's just teasing, you know what he's like."

"Hmm." Fran dug her fork into whatever-it-was, and everyone watched, fascinated, as she lifted it to her mouth. And then stopped. "No. You're probably right, Becky, but I just can't. Lucky I bought a Mars bar on the way to school this morning." She wiped her fork on the edge of the plate and carefully started eating the very furthest chips.

Saima and Megan dug into their healthy salads (Saima's mum was very strict about healthy eating, and Megan took healthy eating very seriously because of football training) and the triplets opened up their lunchboxes.

"Wow!" Katie sounded gobsmacked.

"What?" Annabel asked, as everyone's ears pricked up.

"Mum's actually got our lunches right – look, she's given me peanut butter instead of your disgusting tuna like she usually does. And Becky's actually got her boring old cheese."

"Weird. I'm quite used to having to swap it all round," said Annabel through a mouthful of tuna.

"*Will* you not breathe that stuff over me! Uurgh!" Katie reeled back from tuna fumes, fanning her face in mock disgust.

A nasty snigger floated over from the next table – someone else had obviously been listening in on their conversation. The triplets and their mates united immediately in sending a freezing glare at Amy Mannering. It was a close match between Amy and super-brat Max Carter for the person in their class that they most loved to hate. At that moment Amy was winning – she was nearer.

Amy tossed her long, wavy, strawberry-blonde hair over her shoulder, and the triplets rolled their eyes at each other in disgust. Amy was spoilt, stupid and seriously stuck-up – in their humble opinion. Certain that she had the entire table's attention, Amy continued her conversation with her hangers-on, Emily and Cara.

"Wasn't the girl playing Eliza brilliant? She had *such* a gorgeous voice. My singing teacher" – and here Annabel rolled her eyes again, although secretly she was very jealous, as she would have loved to have singing lessons – "says that I can start working on some of the songs from *My Fair Lady*. I'm so glad we got to see it."

"It was a great trip, Amy. You're so lucky," smarmed Emily. "And we were so close to the stage – you could see everything!"

"The restaurant was fab too," Cara chimed in. She prodded her pizza slice in disgust. "A bit different from this!"

"Oh well, of *course*," Amy said patronizingly, flicking a quick glance round to check that her audience was still with her. "My dad believes birthdays are *so* special. And as I'm an only child – well, he doesn't really have to scrimp and save, does he?" She smirked, carefully looking anywhere but at the triplets. "It's not as if there were *three* of me. . ."

"Thank God," muttered Katie, and the rest of her table burst out laughing.

"There are three of her," Becky pointed out. "Emily and Cara are just Amy without the hair."

"Forget them," advised Saima, firmly. "I'm sick of waiting for you three to tell us. Come on, why were you all so excited this morning? What have you been looking so secretive for all day?"

Amy and co were immediately dismissed as Fran and Megan leant in to hear the news that had made the triplets giggly all through morning classes, and positively hyper at break.

The triplets exchanged glances, their dark blue eyes sparkling with mischief in an expression that made them look more identical than ever. "Weelll. . ." said Annabel slowly.

"What?" snapped Megan and Fran, together.

"It's a secret. Triplets-only. Sorryyy!" cackled Annabel, enjoying their furious faces.

"Annabel," purred Saima sweetly. "We all *know* how ticklish you are. You really, really want to stop messing about and tell us now – don't you?"

"OK! OK!" gasped Annabel, already feeling her hysterical laughter coming on. "Can we tell them?" she begged her sisters.

"I don't see why not – you're not going to be able to shut up about it for much longer anyway," sighed Katie, and Becky nodded.

"Dad's coming home!" squeaked Annabel delightedly, "for all of half-term! Isn't that excellent?"

Saima, Megan and Fran understood

perfectly just how excellent it was. The triplets didn't see their father very often as their parents were divorced and their dad worked abroad as an engineer. At the moment he was working on an irrigation project in Egypt, and the triplets hadn't seen him since early in the summer holidays.

"You'll all have to come round," volunteered Becky unexpectedly. The shyest of the triplets, she tended to leave ideas like this to her sisters. "Fran and Megan haven't met Dad yet," she pointed out, smiling at Fran. The triplets had known Saima from their old school, but they'd only got to know Megan and Fran since starting at Manor Hill that term. Fran shared Becky's complete soppiness over anything furry – especially dogs – and was the first real friend Becky'd had apart from her sisters. She was desperate for Fran to meet Dad and Dad to meet Fran. Describing her new mate in emails just wasn't the same. She was sure they'd get on.

"Definitely!" agreed Katie. "He'll really want to meet you. We can play football, Megan, he's really good, he taught me loads."

The girls beamed at each other, full of their plan. Half-term was only two weeks away – no time at all. The triplets munched their sandwiches happily, and Fran went back to poking dismally at her plate of sheepy bits.

Annabel gazed dreamily over the dining hall, planning shopping trips where Dad bought her and Saima the coolest clothes ever. Slowly chomping a mouthful of tuna and lettuce, her eyes fell on Amy and her thoughts turned to birthdays. Birthdays! Suddenly her eyes snapped wide open, she sat bolt upright and yelped. Or she would have done, except she still had the mouthful of tuna and it went down the wrong way. The yelp came out as a strangled choking noise, and she spat gobbets of tuna all over her sister, then looked at what she'd done in absolute horror (for all of two seconds).

"Bel! Oh, you are so disgusting!" hissed Katie furiously. "Uurrgh, get it *off* me! I'm going to stink of tuna all afternoon. You did that on purpose, you, you—" she became aware of Mrs Andrews's beady eyes zeroing in on their spat, and finished off in a restrained hiss, "you *thing*!"

"Shut up shut up shut up!" chattered Annabel in excitement, flapping her hands around like a mad mime artist, and only just missing Becky who was trying to pass Katie some napkins to mop herself up with. "I've just had The Most Brilliant Idea!"

Chapter Two

Infuriatingly, Annabel refused point-blank to tell anyone but her sisters about her brilliant plan. "Sorry," she told Saima, her best friend, sounding really apologetic for once. "But this really is triplets-only. I just can't. I'll tell you tomorrow, promise. Please don't be cross?" Annabel could be very charming when she wanted, gazing soulfully at Saima and looking as though a cross word would make her burst into tears.

Saima looked miffed, but gave in. She and Megan and Fran knew by now that being friendly with the triplets was great – they were all really sweet, in different ways – but it wasn't like being friends with anybody else. There would always, always be things they didn't understand, things that were "triplets-only". Still, it was worth putting up with, so she grimaced, and shrugged. "OK. But you'd better tell us tomorrow, or else. . ."

"We will. And you'll love it, honestly."

"Excuse me!" butted in Katie. "You haven't told me and Becky either, you know. When do *we* get to hear this idea, Bel?"

"When we get home," replied Annabel firmly. "I'll tell you all about it."

The rest of Monday dragged on as Mondays do. By the end of school Katie and Becky were practically putting Annabel's jacket on for her, they so wanted to get her home and talking. For once they almost wished that Fran and Saima didn't walk home with them most days (Megan lived in the other direction), and they had to try very hard not to show it. When they saw Saima into the turning for her road and they were finally alone, Katie and Becky turned on their sister with positively hungry expressions.

"OK, OK! Don't look at me like that," squeaked Annabel, quite unnerved. They were turning into their road now, and they could see Orlando, one of their two cats, prowling round the garden. He was waiting for Becky to get home and fuss over him, though he always pretended very hard that he just happened to be there at the same time every day. Becky made a kiss-kiss noise, and he gave her a very dignified "You think I'm going to come running?" sort of look before leaping (a bit clumsily, he was rather fat) on to the fence for her to stroke his ears.

"Becky!" snapped Annabel crossly. "I am about to tell you something very important! Why are you messing about with that ginger furball *now*!"

Becky picked Orlando up, and he arranged himself in his favourite position, one paw each side of her neck as though he was hugging her. It gave him the perfect opportunity to direct a pitying glare from his green marble eyes across her shoulder at Annabel – they didn't get on. Becky answered over the top of his head, "I'm not stopping you, Bel. Come on, I'm desperate for a drink. Got the key, Katie?"

Katie burrowed in her jacket pocket for the door key. The triplets' mum was almost always in when they got home, normally doing her translation work at the kitchen table, but they liked having a key to let themselves in – it made them feel very independent.

"Mum! We're home!" Katie yelled, as she shoved the door open with her knee. The triplets' house was quite old, and though it was in no danger of falling down, bits of it did tend to stick or refuse to shut properly. It wasn't a good house for going downstairs to get a drink in the middle of the night – what with the doors and the cats, anyone would be convinced it was haunted before they were halfway.

"Uurgh! Well, I can't tell you now – we need to talk about it before we let Mum in on it." Annabel chucked her jacket at the banisters frustratedly, and didn't notice a conspiratorial look passing between her sisters – and the cat. Annabel should have told them what was going on that afternoon at school. Maybe they should pay her back. This could be fun. . .

"Annabel Ryan! I heard that! Get back there and hang your jacket up in the coat cupboard. What do you think that cupboard is for?"

"Roller skates!" yelled Annabel, rolling her eyes at the other two and scooping up her jacket again. She pulled the door of the understairs cupboard open, and it let out its usual eerie screech. Then she leaned riskily across three pairs of in-line skates, a large bag of woodchip for Becky's guinea pigs and a skateboard, to reach the hooks at the back of the cupboard. "You'd better pass me yours as well while I'm here," she said in a coat-muffled voice. "Ow!"

"What?" asked Katie worriedly, poking her fleece round the door. "Are you OK, Bel?"

"Yeah, I just stabbed myself on that stupid cat-carrier again. Those spiky bits on the door are dangerous."

"Sorry," called Becky, attempting a complicated one-armed jacket-removing manoeuvre without putting down Orlando, who was acting superglued because he knew it would make life difficult. "I think Mum's having one of her tidiness-fits again," she added in a lower voice. "She doesn't normally mind if we put stuff on the banisters."

"It probably all fell on her," came the muffled voice again, accompanied by an impatient hand. "Come *on*, Becky – jacket!"

Katie tugged Becky out of the sleeve she was struggling with and passed the jacket over. Annabel emerged dustily from the cupboard looking like she'd been on a dangerous mission.

"Right," she whispered. "Get juice and

biscuits and then we're going to our room. I'm going to be sick if I don't tell you this idea soon."

"Serves you right," Katie whispered back, grinning. "You shouldn't have been so secretive at lunchtime." Then she led the way into the kitchen where their mum was working at the big pine table. Mrs Ryan translated books from German or French to English, and the other way round. This meant she could do most of her work at home, which made being a mum easier too.

Mum smiled up at the three of them. "Hello! Did you have a good day? Sorry, I've got to finish this bit off, and then we can do tea. Grab yourselves a snack for the minute."

The triplets looked around the kitchen. Yes, apart from the table, which had lots of books piled up on it and several abandoned cups of coffee, the kitchen was looking unusually tidy. Positively shiny, in fact. They sighed. They wouldn't be able to find anything while Mum had this fit on. At least it wasn't likely to last very long. Annabel looked at her mum, who'd just got up to put the kettle on, while Katie grabbed apple juice, and Becky, still one-armed due to Orlando, rootled for biscuits. Mum looked stressed, Annabel thought. Probably too much tidying – the kitchen was hardly recognizable from this morning, and now she came to think of it, the hall had been scarily neat as well.

"Let's go and get changed. OK, Mum? We'll be down in a bit, to help with tea, all right?" And she exchanged meaningful looks with Katie and Becky.

Mum obviously wanted to get back to work – Annabel could tell from the way she kept casting jittery looks at the table – and she didn't complain. "OK, you three. I should have this done in another half an hour, I think."

Annabel shooed her sisters upstairs as fast as she could. They paused worriedly at their bedroom door – no, it was OK, Mum's tidiness mission hadn't got this far, *yet*. Katie gave Becky another conspiratorial look behind Annabel's back, and wandered over to the chair by her bed and started burrowing through the pile of clothes on it.

"What are you doing?" shrieked Annabel, who was jumping up and down with impatience by now.

"Finding some clothes to change into," answered Katie, puzzled. "You said—"

"I didn't mean it! Sit down!" gibbered Annabel. "You two are doing this on purpose, aren't you?"

Becky smirked. "Might be. Might not. . . Oh, come on, Bel, you know you can't keep secrets, 'specially not from us. You shouldn't have tried to make us wait for so long. Maybe we don't *want* to know, now. . ." Then she caught the frustrated, hurt look on her sister's face and melted. "Oh Bel, I'm sorry. We do want to know, don't we, Katie? Look, I'll even put Orlando out of the room, so you can see

I'm really listening." She slipped the cat out of the door and closed it before he'd had time to work out what was going on.

Annabel smiled gratefully. "I wasn't trying to make you wait – well, only a little bit. It's a really good idea, honestly."

Katie and Becky sat down on Katie's bed and gazed up at Annabel, the picture of attention. Annabel took a deep breath, beamed at them and started. "I suddenly thought of it at lunchtime, when those idiots were droning on about Amy's brilliant birthday party. Do you remember what Mum said in July when we were eleven?" (The triplets' birthday was July 4th. American Independence Day – Mrs Ryan always said it had obviously had a real effect on Katie.)

"Oohhh!" breathed Becky and Katie together, starting to realize what Annabel was getting at.

"You see? She said we could have a party if we wanted but then Dad couldn't be there in the summer, except for that one week he was taking us to Wales, so she said why didn't we wait until we'd started at Manor Hill and Dad got some holiday and then we could have Dad at our party and lots of new friends and—"

Her sisters were looking at her goggle-eyed. "Bel, breathe!" snapped Katie. "Honestly, that's the longest sentence I've *ever* heard anybody say in one breath. You're crazy."

"I can see why though," nodded Becky. "It's a great idea, Bel. You're so clever!"

Annabel subsided on to the bed next to them, looking oxygen-starved but happy. She raised her eyebrows hopefully at Katie. Being the oldest of the triplets (by two minutes; Becky was the youngest, a full half-an-hour younger than Annabel) she tended to make most of the decisions – until the other two argued her out of them, anyway.

Katie grinned at her sisters. "It's excellent, Bel. Well done for remembering, I'd forgotten about it completely." She carefully banished the nasty, niggling little voice that was wishing she'd thought of it first, and bounced up from the bed. "Come on! Let's go and tell Mum!"

Chapter Three

The triplets clattered down the stairs, scaring the wits out of Orlando, who was sulking furiously halfway down. He raced down the stairs merely a whisker in front of Annabel and shot into the kitchen. Then he caught sight of the Ryans' other cat, little black Pixie, and stopped dead by his food bowl, giving himself a little shake before assuming the carefree pose of a cat who just happened to be stopping by in case it was nearly tea time.

For once, even Becky wasn't paying much attention to the cats' power struggle. The triplets had far more important things on their minds. "Mum—" they gasped out.

But Mrs Ryan interrupted. "Interesting. I

could have sworn that was what you went upstairs in, but obviously not. . ."

"What?" asked Annabel, completely flummoxed as her head was filled with parties, parties, parties.

"Oh!" said Katie. "Changing! We forgot. We'll do it in a minute. Listen, Mum, Bel's just had the best idea. Go on Bel, tell her!"

Mrs Ryan was all ears now. She'd finished the work she'd been trying to get done, and she liked listening to the triplets' stories about their day when they got home from school. She still found it quite hard not going to pick them up every day, as she had from their primary school, but she knew they loved walking home on their own. She sat down at the table and looked attentive, leaning her chin on her hands. Actually, she looked very like Becky and Katie had, listening to Annabel upstairs. Her blonde hair was curly, and only chin-length, instead of the triplets' long, straight manes, but her blue eyes were exactly the same.

Her daughters ranged themselves along the opposite side of the table, looking remarkably like the same girl three times over, until one spotted the subtle differences: the determined jut of Katie's chin, the mischievous quirk to Annabel's lips, and Becky's thoughtfully twisted eyebrows. They wore their school uniforms differently and tied their hair back in various ways, but their mother always knew them by the way their personalities showed in their faces. It was only difficult when all three were asleep. . .

Annabel started to explain, super-fast again. "Mum, please can we have a birthday party? In half-term when Dad comes home? You said we should wait and invite everyone from Manor Hill, and now we can, and Dad'll be there too!"

Three pairs of blue eyes gazed beseechingly into Mrs Ryan's own. She grinned, and the beseeching eyes turned hopeful. "*Now* I can see why you're all so excited. You nearly broke your necks coming down those stairs." She sighed inwardly as she thought of arranging a party – and clearing up after it. But she *had* promised, and it would be fun, probably, when she wasn't panicking about it. "The first Saturday of half-term, then?" she asked, smiling at the eager faces.

"Yeees!" Annabel jumped up and down, then hurtled round the table to fling herself at her mother, closely followed by Becky and Katie. "Really? We can have a party? Can we invite lots of people? Can we—"

"Calm down!" laughed Mrs Ryan. "Let me have a think about it all. Why don't you go and email your dad? Tell him about it – he'll be just as excited as you, I should think."

The triplets raced off, leaving their mother to make herself yet another strengthening cup of coffee. . .

Back upstairs, lightning-speed changing took place. Katie and Becky threw on jeans and sweatshirts, and Annabel scrambled into a hooded top and her favourite denim skirt and stripy tights. All three of the triplets and their mum shared the computer that lived in the tiny study that had been converted from the loft space right at the top of the house, and the triplets headed up the spiral staircase. Most of the study was filled with Mrs Ryan's work-stuff. She had loads of files – although she wasn't a perfectly organized kind of mum, who had the dates of every school fair and parents' evening imprinted on her brain, she was *very* organized about her work, and the triplets knew not to touch the filing system on pain of death, or at least grounding. They squabbled in a friendly sort of way for the chair in front of the computer-desk, and then Becky and Katie gave it up in favour of Annabel. After all, this was all due to her. They squeezed themselves on to the window sill instead, and Annabel obligingly turned the screen a bit so they could all see.

"Let's read Dad's email again first," suggested

Becky. "We didn't get much chance to look at it this morning. Mum only turned the computer on just before we left."

The triplets had an email address that belonged to all of them – 3ryans@mailserve.co.uk – and one each as well. Dad had sent an email to their main address, and another one to Mum, explaining what was going on. Annabel opened up their email account, and her sisters peered over her shoulder as she checked the inbox.

"Ooh, there's a new message, look!" yelped Becky. "Is it another one from Dad? Oh, don't say he's changed his plans after all, that would be so unfair."

Sure enough, there was another message, and it *was* from Dad. The triplets scanned it anxiously. It was OK! Dad had sent them a picture of a calendar – he said he'd printed it out so he could cross off the days until he came home to see them. "We'll do that too," said Annabel firmly, clicking Print. "Two *weeks*!

That's ages. Maybe we should do something more . . . I don't know, satisfying. Like a thing we could squash for every day gone. Don't you think?" She looked enquiringly at Katie and Becky who were exchanging "Is she anything to do with you?" sort of looks. (It was one they got a lot of practice at.) "It isn't that stupid! Have we got any balloons? Jumping on balloons would be good."

Becky, who wasn't brilliant with unexpected loud noises (she always wore earplugs on Bonfire Night, because she adored fireworks, but couldn't stand the bangs) shuddered. "Well, you're not keeping them in *our* room."

"Baby," jeered Annabel, turning back to the screen. "I can't see Mum being that keen either, though. I'll have to think of something else."

She clicked on Dad's first mail, and her sisters shrugged – it was just Bel being random again. They concentrated on the screen.

From: dryan@fostermarcus.co.uk
   To: 3ryans@mailserve.co.uk
   Subject: Fantastic news!
   Darling ♡ ♡ ♡ !
   Sorry this is a short email – promise I'll send all of you your own personal emails soon – got to go into a meeting any second and I need to mail your mum too. I've just found out that I've got some unexpected leave, and I'm pretty sure it coincides with your half-term. So expect to find me camping on the doorstep on Friday 16th! Loads of love – see you all soon!
   Dad

"It isn't even two weeks, really, Bel," Becky pointed out. "If you don't count today it's only ten days we have to wait."

Annabel gave her a disbelieving look. Patience was not her strong point, and the way she saw it, "only" and "ten days" didn't fit together very well.

Becky poked her in the arm. "Come on, stop looking at me like I'm talking some foreign language, and get typing! What time will it be in Egypt? Will Dad get this before he goes to bed?"

From: 3ryans@mailserve.co.uk
   To: dryan@fostermarcus.co.uk
   Subject: Yay!
   Hey Dad! That's the best news ever! We thought we wouldn't see you till Christmas and now it's way before. And I've had a brilliant idea (it's me, Bel, of course!)

– here both Becky and Katie poked her, but they let her leave it in –

Do you remember we didn't have a birthday party this year? We wanted you to be there for it. Mum says we can have a party in half-term, the day after you get back! So you'd better not be jet-lagged!

Annabel turned round to the pair on the window sill. "I've just remembered something else!" she announced dramatically.

"Congratulations, Bel, it's a record. What?" sighed Katie, impatient to get the message off to Dad.

"Dad gave us spending money in July—"

"Mmm, we know, you bought that skirt with it, so?" Becky sounded puzzled.

"So he didn't send any of us a proper present! He said he'd wait till he was back and we had a party. Don't you remember? Mum said we'd end up with loads too many prezzies around Christmastime – she got quite sniffy about it."

Katie and Becky made faces – they *did* remember. "Quite sniffy" was definitely an understatement. Mum had been worried that the triplets would get spoilt, with both parents competing to get them nice presents. It was something she very definitely wasn't going to let happen.

Katie nodded seriously. "We should definitely remind him. You know what he's, like."

"I don't know," Becky put in. "That might sound – well, as though it's only presents we're bothered about."

"Don't be an idiot, Becky, he knows that's not true. We're just *helping* him. He'd be very upset if he forgot," Bel snapped, feeling a bit guilty. Sometimes Becky was worryingly nice, and it made her feel quite evil by comparison.

Luckily Becky was quite used to her sister's snappy comments, and mostly didn't mind. "Fine, have it your way, you two, as you always do," she sighed, which was quite a sharp retort for her, and made Bel and Katie look at her oddly. Despite her shyness with other people, Becky was definitely sharper these days – she was still the quietest one, but perhaps things were changing.

"We'll do it tactfully, Becky, it'll be fine," Katie assured her.

Becky eyed Bel meaningfully.

"I can be tactful! Oh, all right. You'd better tell me what to say."

After quite a lot of bickering and deleting, they ended up with what they all agreed was a masterpiece of tactful parent-management.

We haven't worked out what sort of party
we want to have yet. We need to think fast.
Any ideas? It's so exciting – we really
missed having a party in the summer,
'cause normally it means we get loads of
presents!!!! Just before the holidays, which
is brilliant timing. We've got to go and
help Mum make tea now, she's yelling up
the stairs. Write back soon! Love Bel,
Katie and Becky xxxxxxxx

And as Annabel said, "If that doesn't make him think about presents, nothing will."

Chapter Four

On Tuesday morning the triplets were even madder and bouncier than usual. Normally this would have driven Mrs Ryan demented, but she made allowances for party-madness. Actually, the triplets were so desperate to get to school and tell everyone about their party that their craziness was directed towards getting out of the house as fast as possible. The only problem was that Becky and Bel ate their breakfast so fast they had the hiccups all the way to school, and Katie couldn't stop sniggering at them. Despite their rush, super-organized Saima was there before them, staked out by the huge chestnut tree in the playground that was unofficial territory for the triplets and their mates. Annabel positively danced up to her, still hiccupping, and trailing the other two like follow-my-leader.

"Saima, we have got the *best* news!" She managed to get this out in a rush before the next hiccup — Saima practically had to lip-read it and it was a good ten seconds before she could translate what Annabel had said.

"So? Tell me! What is it? Oh, you've got hiccups!"

Annabel gave her a Look. "Ob — hic — viously. Don't laugh. It's been — hic — ages. Becky too."

Becky nodded at Saima, and gave a kind of full-body twitch. It was her version of hiccups — no noise, just the bounce.

Saima went into capable mode. "Honestly, you three are useless."

"*I* haven't got hiccups!" protested Katie, indignantly.

"No, but you haven't sorted out these two, have you?"

"I did try." Katie sniggered again. She was also feeling crazy this morning, and her normally sensible attitude had gone walkabout. Her method of stopping her sisters' hiccups had been walking fast to get round the corners ahead of them, and then popping out to do her very realistic impression of Sully from *Monsters, Inc.* Annabel and Becky were now irritable hiccupy nervous wrecks, and Katie was as close to hysterical as she ever got.

Saima fixed Annabel and Becky with a hypnotic stare, and said sternly. "Look at me, you two! Now, what's this?" she waved something deliciously familiar under their noses.

"Mars – hic – bar!" Now they were drooling hiccupy nervous wrecks.

"Exactly," purred Saima, "and the next one of you two to hiccup gets it."

"Whaaat!" squeaked Katie, shocked. "You're *giving* them a Mars bar? What about me? Please, Saima, I'm starving, can I have some too?"

Becky and Annabel exchanged smug looks.

Weirdly, they'd been hic-ing and bouncing completely in time up till now – they generally did if two of them or all three had hiccups. It was one of the triplet things that freaked people out. Dad thought it was hilarious– "Even your stomachs are identical!" They could share the Mars bar and enjoy waving choice bits at Katie after all her unsympathetic monster impressions. But for some reason they were now in a kind of suspended animation, tensely anticipating the next hiccup, which wasn't happening.

Saima watched with a funny little smile on her face, and Katie calmed down almost completely. How could they all be so wound up waiting for hiccups, for goodness' sake?

A full two minutes later, Saima very deliberately put the Mars bar away in her rucksack.

"Awww, Saima!" wailed Annabel. "That's torture!"

"You hiccup, you get it. And I can tell fake

hiccups so don't try," added Saima, noting the evil gleam in Annabel's eyes. "You're cured, both of you."

"That's brilliant," said Katie. "Does it always work?"

"Not so well after the first few times," admitted Saima. "But I thought it was a pretty safe bet. Now, news please!"

At that moment, Fran and Megan dashed up. "Hello! What's going on? Can you tell us your idea yet, Bel?" asked Fran eagerly, dark-green eyes sparkling with anticipation.

"Yes, go on, what is it?" begged Megan.

Annabel drew a deep breath, loving the attention. "*We* are going to have a party," she announced dramatically. Then the triplets gazed happily round at their best friends, who were reacting very satisfyingly, jumping about and asking excited questions.

"When?"

"Who are you going to invite?"

"What sort of party?"

"Well," said Annabel, plumping herself down on one of the huge twisted roots that made the chestnut tree such a good place to gather, and patting the seat-like bumps next to her, "we don't really know what sort of party yet. Mum said she wanted to have a think about it, and consider her budget." Annabel made a face. "Parties are expensive."

Katie nodded. "Sorry, you lot, but I don't think we'll all be going to see any fancy London musicals. Have a think, though. Suggestions welcome!"

"Oh, don't be silly," said Megan, poking Katie (who was practically sitting on her knee) and making her squawk. "It doesn't have to be fancy. You could do loads of things. Just loads of us hanging round your living room and watching DVDs would be cool. Why don't you have a sleepover?"

"That *is* a good idea," said Katie, thoughtfully. "What do you think?" She wriggled herself round to look at Annabel and Becky.

Becky nodded, enthusiastically, but Annabel didn't look convinced. "I do like the sleepover idea, I'd just like to do something more exciting – and then have everyone sleeping over, maybe."

The bell rang then, and the discussion stopped until registration – where the triplets and their friends got so excited that Miss Fraser had to keep shushing them and the rest of the class were absolutely desperate to know what was going on. By break, the whole class knew that the Ryan triplets were having a party, and they were buzzing with excitement. The big question was, who was going to be invited?

The triplets weren't sure and said so – it depended on what kind of party it was. "After all," Annabel pointed out to her friend Matt in history, "you wouldn't want to come to a girly sleepover and do makeovers and watch DVDs, would you?"

"Depends on the DVDs," Matt said, but he got the point.

"One thing's for definite, though," Katie

leaned over to say to Annabel. "We are *so* not inviting THEM!" Them was quite obviously Amy, Emily and Cara, who were trying very hard to look as though they couldn't care less, but were clearly listening to the party gossip. David, who sat with them in history and didn't know that many people yet, was looking gloomy. Yet again, Amy and co hadn't exchanged a word with him this morning. It seemed likely that they wouldn't talk to him all year.

Annabel grinned back. "Too right. And not him, either," she added in a whisper, jabbing her thumb at Max, who sat close to Katie (unfortunately).

Max apparently had ears like a really ugly species of bat, because he snapped back, "I wouldn't want to come to your stupid party anyway!"

Katie looked down her nose at him, which was impressive because he was taller than her. "Were we talking to you?"

"No, but—"

"I thought not. Shut up, Toadbreath."

"Katherine." A pleasant, slightly Scottish voice broke into the conversation.

"Er, yes, Miss Fraser?" quavered Katie, hoping that Miss Fraser was going miraculously deaf in her not-very-old age.

"I gather that you and your sisters are having a party. I suggest that if you'd like to be out of detention in time to go to it, you attempt to behave a little more politely to the rest of your history group. Mmm?"

"Yes, Miss Fraser." And Katie was completely silent for the rest of the lesson.

The rest of the day passed in a haze of more and more crazy party suggestions from practically everyone the triplets knew. Fiona, one of the triplets' friends from their old school, was trying to convince Becky that they should have a fancy-dress party where everyone came as their favourite film stars, when the bell went.

The triplets didn't go home together on Tuesdays, as Saima and Annabel went to ballet class at the leisure centre after school. The two of them wandered over to the class, still turning over party ideas.

"I suppose it's difficult being a triplet when you have to arrange this sort of thing. You can't all have exactly what you want," Saima mused.

"Mmm," replied Annabel vaguely, glossing over Saima's comment. She had so many fabulous plans for this party, she didn't want to think about not getting them. "I'm sure it'll be OK. I think we'd all really like a disco. I wonder how much it costs? We wouldn't need a proper DJ, I suppose, but it would be really cool to have real disco lights. Or a glitterball!"

Saima was won over immediately. "Oooh, yes. Then you could have a kind of glittery theme for the whole party!"

They were off. By the time they'd got to the leisure centre, and changed into their leotards and ballet shoes, they even had the food organized – little iced cakes, because they could put edible glitter on them and Annabel loved the idea of eating glitter. "And maybe some crisps," she added as an afterthought.

Saima could only nod back, as the class was just starting. Their teacher, Mrs Flowers, had actually been a professional ballet dancer, but she'd explained to them that ballet was a very difficult career – you couldn't go on being a ballet dancer for all that long, it was just too demanding once you were older. So lots of dancers went into teaching instead. After the warm-up exercises, Mrs Flowers split the class in two so that they could practise the sequence of steps that they'd been learning for the last couple of weeks. Annabel and Saima were in different groups, so Annabel sat on the long bench at the side of the room, watching as the other half of the class went through the steps. It was very impressive: fifteen girls, dressed identically in black leotards with pink gauze wrap-around skirts, and doing exactly the same steps. *Well, almost*, Annabel thought, as she noticed Lucy in the back row forgetting what she was supposed to be doing with her arms.

Saima was in the front row. She was very good at ballet, and all sorts of dancing. She went to Indian dancing classes as well, which she said weren't at all like ballet, because she had to move in a totally different way, and do lots of complicated things with her hands. And the costumes were brilliant – she'd let Annabel try them on with her, and said that one day she'd try and teach her some steps too. *Maybe in half-term?* Annabel wondered. The group in the centre finished their dance, and Annabel and the others perked up – it was about to be their turn.

"Good. Watch those arms, please, girls. Very expressive hands, Saima dear, lovely." "Expressive" was Mrs Flowers's favourite word, that and "again" – as in, "You can be much more expressive than that, girls, do it again."

For once, Annabel didn't mind when ballet was over. She'd been distracted by glitter all through the class, and thinking more about her favourite music than the Chopin they were dancing to. Luckily, being in a glittery, party mood hadn't hurt her dancing at all. In fact Mrs Flowers had said that her step-sequence had a lovely carefree feeling. "Lovely" was another of her favourite words.

Annabel couldn't wait to get home; for a start Mum and Katie and Becky would probably have got tea ready, and she was starving. Ballet might look delicate and graceful, but it was *very* hard work. More importantly, though, she wanted to tell them all about her brilliant plans for the party.

Katie and Becky had spent the walk home in a party daze as well, although not quite as glittery a one as Annabel's. Katie was wondering how much it would cost to hire the swimming pool at the leisure centre – it had great inflatable things you could jump off, and a water-chute. Or what about going to see a football match?

"Becky!" She poked her sister in the ribs, jolting her out of a daydream. "Becky, wake up! You'd like to go to a football match, wouldn't you? I bet Dad would take us for a birthday treat."

"Are you mad? A football match? You and Megan would love it, and I s'pose I wouldn't mind that much, but can you imagine Bel? And Saima? They'd freak."

"No they wouldn't! It would be fun, they'd just need to make a bit of an effort and I bet they'd enjoy it."

Becky sniggered, imagining Annabel and Saima in football scarves (bound to be the wrong team colour to go with their outfits). "Katie, the only thing Bel knows about football is that she thinks all the players have stupid hair. She – would – *hate* – it! Wouldn't she?"

Katie grumped along for a bit. She didn't want to be convinced, but Becky was right – she *couldn't* see Annabel or dainty Saima enjoying a footie match. Really she'd only been arguing back for the principle of the thing. Annabel was even going off their shambolic kickabouts in the garden these days. Katie went back to her first idea. "How about a swimming party? With the big chute and everything? Wouldn't you like that?" she coaxed.

"Mmm. . ." Becky sounded thoughtful. "Mmm, yes. That would be cool. And maybe we could have a sleepover afterwards. Mum would let us, I bet she would."

Becky didn't want to tell anyone, even her triplet, what she'd been daydreaming about for their party. It was too silly. She'd started off vaguely wondering if they could do something that involved animals, but she just wasn't sure that Katie or Annabel would be happy with a trip to London Zoo. They'd been once before with Auntie Janet, Mum's sister who lived in London, and loved it, but that was a couple of years ago. Besides, Becky wasn't sure about keeping really big, wild kinds of animals in cages. Guinea pigs she didn't have a problem with (luckily, or else there'd be four homeless guinea pigs wandering around their garden) but lions and polar bears needed more room than a zoo. This was where she'd got really over the top. Polar bears. . . It would be the best party ever – she and Katie and Annabel and their friends, wearing big (fake) furry coats on sledges pulled by teams of gorgeous cuddly husky dogs, speeding across the Arctic snowfields to go polar-bear-watching. Mmm. . . Katie's football match idea had brought her back to earth with a bump (the huskies all ended up tail-deep in a snowdrift).

Back in the real world again, a swimming

party *did* sound nice. Basically Becky didn't mind that much what kind of party they had. She just wanted all her new friends having fun together, and obviously some presents would be good. She smiled to herself as she thought back to the beginning of term, when she'd been so upset about Katie and Annabel making new friends. How could she have been so silly?

Chapter Five

"What's for tea? I'm *sooo* hungry!" Annabel demanded of Katie who'd opened the front door for her. Remembering Mum's new regime, she slung her ballet bag and jacket into the cupboard under the stairs (which was rapidly becoming the home for any untidyable mess).

"Spag Bol. You'd better go and change, you've got to wear that sweatshirt three more days before it gets washed, and you and Spag Bol are a disaster area. Find something that's already grubby." Katie stood with her hands on her hips, looking stern. "And don't you want your ballet stuff *washing*?"

"All right, *Mum*!" sniggered Annabel, dumping her rucksack halfway up the stairs, which she didn't think Mum could complain about as that was where she did her homework – she claimed it was easier to think on the stairs. Then she retrieved her tights and leotard and raced up to their room to dump them in the washing basket and get changed – Katie was right, she didn't want to be wearing a tomatoey sweater for the rest of the week. Throwing on jeans and a pretty red T-shirt (careful tomato camouflage) that she'd already managed to chuck a spot of yoghurt down at the weekend, Annabel dashed downstairs, eager to tell Mum and Katie and Becky how gorgeously she'd worked everything out.

Unfortunately, things didn't quite go to plan. For a start, when she got into the kitchen, Katie and Becky were deep in discussion of something else – swimming or something, *boooring!* – but they seemed pretty excited about it.

"What do you think, Bel?" Katie asked her eagerly.

"'Bout what?" Annabel hadn't really been listening.

"The party, of course!" Katie sounded impatient.

"All right, keep your hair on! Wow, you're so snappy, I only asked. Anyway, that's what I wanted to tell you all about. Saima and I have worked it all out, it's going to be fab. The only thing is, Mum, we absolutely *have* to get a glitterball from somewhere, it's kind of the theme of the whole party. And I had this totally brilliant idea, but I wasn't sure you'd agree. . ." Annabel turned pleading eyes on her mother. "Can we repaint the living room? You know you can get that cool glitter paint? It would be amazing, really. You wouldn't have to lift a finger, Mum, we'll do it, easy. Won't we?" Annabel looked happily at Katie and Becky, expecting glowing enthusiasm. She didn't get it. Becky looked worried, scared almost, and Katie was just plain scowling.

"What exactly are you wittering on about,

Bel?" she said. "What's glitter got to do with anything?"

Annabel shoved Saima's comment about not always getting what you wanted when you were a triplet to the back of her brain and stood on it hard. She obviously just hadn't explained properly because she was so excited. Her sisters would love the plan once they'd really got it. She beamed determinedly at them, and patiently started again. "Our party's going to be a disco, OK? And we get a glitterball for when we're dancing, and the whole party is glittery, that's why I want to paint the walls, I showed you the stuff in the DIY shop, remember? We can have glittery cakes, and you can both borrow my glitter nail polish, it'll be so cool. . ." She faltered to a stop. Katie's expression was not saying it was going to be cool, and Becky was doing that weird thing where she gnawed on her knuckles. Mum just looked as though she was awaiting developments. "What's the matter?" Annabel asked, confused.

"You worked all this out at ballet?"

"Yes, well, on the way there—"

"With Saima?" Katie folded her arms. All pretence of eating tea had stopped now.

"Yeah, the glitter theme was her idea, don't you think it's brilliant?"

"Oh yes, it's *great*," but Katie's voice wasn't fitting her words.

"Oh, good, I wasn't sure if you—"

"For you. And Saima. Where exactly do me and Becky fit into the Glitter Party?" Suddenly Katie's voice rose to a yell. "Were you even going to let us be there?"

"Katie!" Mum said in a warning voice, and Katie shut up and just glared at her sister, obviously too furious to talk.

Annabel, on the other hand, was furious and very talkative. "What is your problem!" she snarled. "Of course you'd be there, this is our party, what's wrong with you today? I worked out all this stuff for you—"

"No, you didn't!" Katie was holding herself

58

back from yelling, which resulted in an angry hiss. "You worked it out for *you*. This is a party for *you*, not us. You couldn't even be bothered to listen to mine and Becky's ideas, you just walked in and told us it was all settled! Well, it's not, because I think your 'glittery disco' sounds rubbish and I wouldn't have a party like that if you paid me!"

"Your ideas! You mean that *stupid* swimming thing you were droning on about was supposed to be a party? Wow, swimming, how *very* exciting. It's a good thing you've got me to arrange everything for you, because you are a boring *sad* person, Katie."

"Right, I've had enough of this," Mrs Ryan snapped. "You're behaving appallingly, and I see absolutely no reason to spend a great deal of time and money arranging a party for a pack of ungrateful little horrors. You can't agree what to do, so there's a simple solution – you won't have a party at all."

"But Mum—"

"Oh, that's not fair—"

"Be quiet!" It was Mrs Ryan's super-scary, "be quiet now if you ever want to leave this house again except for school" voice, and they shut up instantly. Their mum fixed them with a laser-beam glare until she was certain they weren't even considering answering back. Then she looked at Becky whose eyes were full of tears, partly because she'd really been looking forward to the party, but mostly because she hated it when their friendship got split up like this. It didn't happen often, but when it did, she felt it as though it was actually hurting her. "I'm sorry, love. I know you weren't arguing, but it'll just have to be unfair on you, I'm afraid. Now, all of you, finish your tea and then go upstairs. I don't want to see you or hear you for the rest of the evening."

They ate mechanically, hardly tasting the pasta, their minds boiling with the unfairness and disaster of it all. Katie and Annabel were each convinced it was entirely the other's fault; and Becky was seething at both of them for being so stupid. As soon as all three of them had finished, Mum gave a pointed look towards the kitchen door and they slunk off upstairs.

As soon as they got to their bedroom, Katie and Annabel turned on each other again. "Now look what you've done!" Katie started. "Great! Now we can't have a party at all, just because you had to be so stupid and selfish!"

"*I'm* selfish? I like that! That party would have been brilliant, and you had to go ruin it because you wanted to go swimming." Annabel said "swimming" with absolute venom.

"Oh, shut up!" sighed Becky.

"Oh, I'm sorry, Little Miss Perfect!" said Annabel nastily. "Darling Becky never argues, does she?"

"Don't be a cow, Bel. There's no point taking it out on me. Just stop it, both of you. It's pointless, you've done it, so stop bickering. OK, so Annabel shouldn't have planned everything with Saima, but we were planning a swimming party, weren't we, Katie, without Bel being there. And actually, I thought bits of Bel's idea sounded cool."

"I suppose so," growled Katie, still grumpy, but not furious any more.

"And I don't know what your problem with swimming is suddenly," Becky said, rounding on Annabel. "You *like* swimming!"

"I know, but swimming or a disco! No contest! Do you think Mum really meant it?"

"Sounded like it," said Becky sadly. "I s'pose she might change her mind if we're little angels for a few days – maybe."

Annabel stretched out on her bed, and propped her chin on her hands. Mum was really busy with work and she'd been tired and distracted for the last few days. Maybe she'd come round when things calmed down?

Katie and Becky joined Annabel on her bed, to feel depressed in unison, and Annabel rolled more on to her side and took the band off the end of Katie's tight plait. She unravelled it and started to redo it in lots of tiny ones. Becky joined in, grabbing a box of stretchy bands from Annabel's bedside table.

Katie gave an irritable twitch, and said she wished they'd mess around with their own hair, but it was more for show than anything else, and when Becky poked her in a "lie down" kind of way, and Annabel told her to shut up and keep still, she subsided, grumbling, but enjoying the attention, liking all being friends again.

"You should wear your hair like this, you know," Annabel told her about ten minutes later. "It suits you. You shouldn't always just scrape it straight back."

"I suppose it's OK," admitted Katie, staring into the mirror. "So much fuss, though. And it flicks about everywhere." She shook her head to demonstrate and the plaits whisked round her face. "See?"

"Yeah, well, the simple answer is not to do

that, dimwit. Anyway, I've just thought" – Annabel was standing by the door – "Dad might have replied to our email. Let's go and see."

Mum hadn't *said* they had to stay in their room, but the triplets had a feeling that was what she'd meant, so they sneaked up the staircase to the study on fairy-feet. Then Annabel and Katie perched on half the chair each, and Becky knelt beside them, all peering impatiently at the screen as the computer chugged maddeningly slowly through its warm-up routine. Dad *had* answered and Mum was right, he sounded really excited, positively gleeful. He assured them he wouldn't have even the slightest hint of jet lag – in fact he said he'd dance the night away, which made Annabel glance triumphantly at the other two. He promised he hadn't forgotten their present, either. All in all, it should have been a really brilliant email for the triplets to read – instead it was absolutely infuriating. All this excitement about a party that wasn't going to happen!

"Oh well," said Katie gloomily. "Do you think we'd better tell him it's all off?"

"No, leave it for a bit — you never know," Annabel advised, hopefully. "Come on, it's too depressing. Let's go and do something else."

"Mmm, homework," Becky agreed sadly. "We've got loads, remember? Come on." And she led the miserable trio back downstairs to fetch their stuff. Then she and Katie headed back up to their room with their piles of books, and Annabel settled herself on the stairs to make ugly faces at her history homework.

Chapter Six

Mum was still quiet and tight-lipped next morning, so the triplets tiptoed round her, and got themselves out of the way as quickly as possible. The group round the tree was dismal that morning, after the triplets broke the news. They didn't really go into details, just said that they'd had a row with their mum and it looked like the party was off.

"And the worst thing is," Annabel spat, scowling across the playground at Amy and co, "I was really looking forward to *not* inviting them. They're going to gloat like mad, I can tell."

"*So* not fair," agreed Saima, shaking her head sadly. "She just didn't deserve a party."

"You never know," said sensible Fran, putting an arm round Becky and giving her a quick hug, "your mum might change her mind. Anyway, there'll be other parties. My mum promised I could have a sleepover soon. It is a total pain, though," she added, catching a triumphant gleam in Amy's eyes as she whispered excitedly to Emily and Cara. How on earth could she have found out already?

But they had. The triplets and their friends were back by the chestnut tree at break, gloomily sharing each other's crisps, when Amy and her followers sauntered by. Amy stopped by them, folded her arms and flicked back her strawberry-blonde hair. "So, I hear your party's off then?" she sneered. "Not that I'm convinced you were ever *having* a party. It all sounded a little bit too – convenient. Don't you think?" she asked Emily and Cara, who were standing on either side of her, slightly behind, like evil henchmen in some bad film.

"Definitely," sniggered Emily.

"They *so* made it up." Cara nodded sagely.

Amy smirked down at the triplets, who were speechless. "Oh, look. They're too upset to speak. Poor babies," she said, her voice like poisoned honey.

Annabel gathered her wits and smiled up at Amy. "I don't know why you're bothered," she replied, equally sweet, "it's not as if we'd ever have invited someone as stupid as you anyway." Then she feigned complete interest in her nails, and ignored Amy's furious face. Katie and Becky and the others told her afterwards that they'd never seen anyone go that colour – sort of bright white, but with scary pink slashes over the cheekbones.

"Oh, Bel, it was classic," giggled Saima. "She is so going to kill you horribly if she ever thinks she can get away with it though. You'd better be careful, she's really nasty."

They were totally cheered up for the rest of the morning and they all trooped into French, last lesson before lunch, still cackling every time they saw Amy.

Becky suddenly sobered up. "Oh no, I completely forgot, I meant to go over my vocab again at break. I'm sure I've forgotten those stupid verbs, even if I did spend ages on it last night."

"You'll be fine," Katie told her. "I tested you, remember? You knew it loads better than I did."

"Umm, Katie? Becky?" Annabel's voice was very quiet. "What are you talking about?"

Five faces turned to look at her in horror.

"Oh, Bel!" Saima gasped. "You didn't forget?"

"Forget what?" wailed Annabel in a panic. "What are we supposed to have learned?"

"Oh, just *all* the French vocab we've done so far!" snapped Katie. "Annabel Ryan, how could you be such a total and utter fruitbat? Mr Hatton kept reminding us all of last week! Have you really not learned *any* of it?"

"No," whispered Annabel huskily, her eyes

huge and dark blue with panic. "I'm dead! What am I going to do?"

There was nothing her sisters could do to help – not even a last-minute crash course in how to say "I am eleven years old" and "I am from England" in French, because Mr Hatton had already arrived and was chivvying everybody to sit down so he could dole out test papers. Katie noticed Max murmuring to one of his mates, and pointing out Annabel. Great! He'd heard them talking about it. (He gave her a horrible smirking look as he noticed her watching.) She was so worried about Annabel that she couldn't summon up much more than a disdainful stare, and it didn't seem to have much effect. Now Max was bound to do all he could to make things worse.

The Test (it definitely had capital letters) was long, a page of A4 with two huge columns of words and phrases, one in French that they had to translate, and one in English that they had to find the French for.

Although they were normally very honest, Katie and Becky would have helped Annabel with the test – how could they not, when she looked so upset? But Mr Hatton was notorious at Manor Hill for being massively-strict when it came to tests. He gave out detentions if anyone so much as flickered an eyelash in someone else's direction, and he was already convinced that the triplets had some kind of ESP that could beam the French for rabbit halfway across the classroom. Becky and Katie were trying like mad (why did all those triplet mind-reading stories never work when they most needed them?) but Annabel still had her nose about five centimetres from her test paper and was clearly trying not to cry. At times like this, wearing her long, thick blonde hair loose was very useful – she could hide behind it.

Mr Hatton gave them twenty minutes to do the test, and then made everyone swap papers so they could mark each other's. Megan looked

down at Annabel's answers, slightly horrified –
there practically weren't any. Annabel was
sitting up a bit more now, but completely
behind a curtain of hair. She'd even taken her
clips out, so that it hung straight down round
her face. A hand emerged from behind her hair
to mark Fran's answers (mostly right).

Mr Hatton's other mean habit was making
people tell him their test scores out loud – he
had to put them down in his marks book, but
he could easily have gathered them in and
checked for himself. Instead he went round
the room, rolling his eyes and muttering to
himself at the marks.

"Francesca? Thirty-five – at last, someone
who did actually learn the work properly.
Rebecca? Thirty-four, yes, good. Katherine?
Thirty, try harder next time, please. Annabel?
I *beg* your pardon?"

"Six," muttered Annabel again, *really* on the
verge of crying by now.

"Six. I see. . . Did I ask for comment?" He

suddenly turned on the rest of the class, who had erupted in a wave of amazed muttering and – from certain very predictable corners – stifled sniggering. "See me at the end of the lesson. Right, the rest of you. Megan?" And so it went on.

There wasn't much time until the end of the lesson, and when the bell went everyone surged to their feet, eager for lunch and the opportunity to go and be pleasantly shocked at people who managed to mess up their birthday parties and get six out of forty in a test on the *same day*. The triplets stayed put. "See you in the dining hall," Katie murmured to the others as they straggled out, still looking anxiously at Annabel.

Mr Hatton turned from the desk where he was packing up his books and things, and raised his eyebrows in a typically French–teacherish way. "Correct me if I'm wrong, but I have a strong suspicion that I asked for *Annabel* to stay behind to explain her disgraceful test results. The other two, wait outside." Katie and Becky shuffled out sheepishly, leaving Annabel staring at the desk – and the test paper. Mr Hatton picked it up between finger and thumb, as though it might bite him, and waved it at Annabel. "Did you learn any of this?"

The hairy thing that was Annabel shook itself – no.

"Well, at least you're not stupid enough to pretend that you did. Something more important came up, did it?"

The hair shook again, and a small mutter emerged. "Just forgot."

"I see. Well, you'll be in detention on Friday, doing the test again, and if you don't get at least thirty, you'll keep on taking it until you do. Clear?"

The hair nodded violently.

"Good. Detention slip. Don't *forget* to get it signed by your mother."

*

Outside the classroom, Katie and Becky were desperately trying to listen through the door, but Mr Hatton had shut it firmly behind them and it was no good. At last it clicked open, and the hair trailed out. They took one look and realized that emergency measures were needed. Katie grabbed Annabel's schoolbag, and they took one arm each, practically carrying their sister towards the girls' toilets, where they installed themselves on the big window sill above the radiator (luckily not occupied by gossiping make-up-swapping Year Tens for once) and hugged Annabel between them. The triplets were in that small, fortunate group of people who didn't look completely awful when they cried. When Katie swept Annabel's hair back off her face she was streaming tears, but apart from that she just had a fetchingly pink nose. Becky dug around in her rucksack till she found a packet of tissues, and for five minutes they handed them to Annabel, patted her heaving shoulders and murmured soothing nothings. It took about that long for Annabel to start calming down enough to sniff, "Thanks," when the next tissue appeared.

"Try and make that one last, Bel," Becky advised, "you've gone through the whole packet and there's never any loo paper in here."

"'K."

"You are a twit, Bel," said Katie affectionately. "Did he put you in detention?"

"Mm-hm. Got to do the test again," heaved her sister, still half sobbing. "And Mum has to sign a slip. She'll be so cross."

"She won't," they assured her, hopefully, exchanging glances. Unless she was still in that twitchy mood because of all the work she had on, of course. . . Katie looked down at Annabel, and felt a wave of elder-by-two-minutes-sisterly sympathy roll over her. It was mean of her, she knew, but she couldn't help it – she felt so much *better* when Annabel was being useless and relying on her to sort things out.

Super-efficient party-organizing Annabel had been a nasty shock.

"Do you want any lunch, Bel?" she asked.

"Don't know. Maybe a bit."

"Come on, then." Katie slid down from the window sill, and they soaked a few paper towels in water for Annabel to wash her face.

"Honestly, Bel, if you smile and look normal, no one would ever know you've been crying," Becky assured her. "Just think back to before school and the look on Amy Mannering's face – that'll cheer you up."

They headed off to the dining hall, Katie and Becky still treating Annabel as though she were a delicate piece of china.

"You all right, Bel?" Saima asked anxiously as they slid into their seats, and all the others looked at her worriedly.

"I'm fine. Really. I've got to do the test again, that's all." Embarrassed, Annabel grabbed her sandwiches, and did a very good impression of someone who thought tuna and lettuce was the most interesting thing she'd ever seen.

Katie and Becky heaved sighs of relief. Hopefully things were OK. Annabel was looking much better, they could just forget about it — until they got her home and could start stuffing her brain with French vocab, that was.

Or maybe not. "Oh no, Becky, look," Katie murmured. "No, over *there*, idiot. Max! He's definitely coming this way."

Without realizing it, they both fluffed themselves up like cats, stiffening their shoulders, tensing all over. Max was definitely coming over to be nasty. He stood on the other side of their table, next to Saima, who put down her first spoonful of chocolate pudding and glared up at him in disgust.

"What do *you* want?" she snapped.

Max ignored her, sat down in a spare seat and grinned at Annabel who was still clutching her sandwich and looking at him like a rabbit caught in headlights. She knew he was about to be horrible, and she was still feeling too upset and shaky to stand up to him.

"Don't look so worried, Annabel. Even *you* can remember the French for that," he nodded at her lunch. "*Un sandwich*. Easy. Go on, repeat after me. . ."

After all their desperate mind-reading attempts in the French lesson, it was typical that Katie and Becky should be able to manage it now. One split-second glance at each other, and they knew what they were going to do. Becky sprang up from her seat, muttering something about having lost her bag, and oh no where was it? (Under the table, very obviously.) As soon as Becky had effectively masked them from Miss Fraser, who was on lunch-duty, Katie went into action. Leaning over the table, she reached out to Saima. "Oh, Saima, look, you've dropped custard down your front. Here, let me – oh *no!*" This was a very over the top, theatrical exclamation, as she waved wildly at the nonexistent custard – and swiped the entire chocolatey bowlful off the table and down Max's front and all over his trousers.

"Oooh, Katie, look what you've *done*!" cooed Becky. "*Poor* Max, it looks awful. . ."

"Max, I'm really sorry, do you want to borrow my PE kit to change into?" asked Katie in an ever-so-concerned voice. "I don't know *how* I could be so clumsy!"

Max was speechless – for about ten seconds. Then he stood up, ignoring the sniggers as people caught sight of the state he was in. He looked round for the teacher on duty. "Miss Fraser! Miss Fraser!" The triplets' class teacher came over, trying hard to wipe the smile from her face – Max did look very funny.

"Oh, dear! What happened, Max, did you have an accident?"

"No!" snapped Max furiously. "They did it on purpose, I know they did."

Miss Fraser raised her eyebrows. "Really? And who is 'they'?"

"Them! Those triplets, they spilt it all over me!"

Miss Fraser looked round at the triplets, who were looking mildly surprised – as though they had no idea what he was wittering on about, but then this *was* Max, and really, what could one expect?

"Katie? Is this true?"

"No, Miss Fraser!" Katie sounded hurt. She couldn't act as well as Annabel, but when it was absolutely necessary, she could pull something like this off. "It was Saima's pudding, and I did knock it over, but it wasn't on purpose. I told Max, I said I was really sorry. I said he could borrow my tracksuit trousers if he wanted – he's going to need something. Shall I go and ask Mrs Hagan for some paper napkins?"

Miss Fraser surveyed the triplets again: Katie looked mildly embarrassed at having caused all this mess, Becky was looking worriedly at the state of Max's clothes, and Annabel looked quiet and pale – not at all like someone who'd just pulled off the kind of stunt that Max was claiming. In fact, it was lucky for the triplets that Annabel was still feeling a bit fragile, otherwise she would have been having trouble holding back her giggles.

"No, I think Max needs to go and change. Really Max, if it was an accident, and Katie has apologized, I'm afraid it's just one of those things. Have you got your PE kit in school to wear instead?"

Max growled something vaguely like yes. He knew perfectly well that it hadn't been an accident, but there was no way he could prove it. He stomped off, a wave of tittering following him through the dining hall. Miss Fraser returned to the other side of the hall.

"Sorry, Saima," chuckled Katie. "It was too good to miss. I'll go and get you some more pudding."

"No, it's OK, it wasn't that nice. I can't think of a better place for it, really, unless you'd got it in his hair. . ." Saima sounded dreamy as she considered the possibilities of Max with his hair stiff with school custard.

"You all right, Bel?" Becky asked anxiously. "You're awfully quiet."

Annabel grinned. "I'm fine. You two are brilliant. That was almost worth messing up a French test for!"

Chapter Seven

Max turned up for afternoon registration in his tracksuit bottoms and a chocolate-stained sweater. He had to explain what had happened to every teacher they had that afternoon — it just got funnier each time the triplets heard it, although they had to make an effort to look apologetic to keep up the pretence that it had all been an accident.

Wednesdays were practice evenings for the girls' junior football team. Katie had been going along to these for a couple of weeks now, with Megan, because Mrs Ross was trying them out for places on the team, Katie as a forward player, and Megan as goalie. It was pretty impressive to be considered in their first term at the school. The only other girl in their year that Mrs Ross had picked out was Cara, Amy's friend. As far as Katie and Megan could see, being good at football was the only decent thing about her.

Mrs Ross was really nice, but she made them work incredibly hard, and after an hour's practice Katie and Megan were exhausted, and Katie was thinking longingly of going home and having a bath, she was so muddy. Mrs Ross collared her as she was dragging her mud-encrusted football boots towards the changing rooms.

"Katie! You did very well today, I was pleased with you. I'm going to do some swapping around in the team for the next few matches, and I'd like you to play. OK?"

Katie was speechless. OK? It was brilliant! She'd thought next term, *maybe*, she'd get a game, but not yet.

"I'm going to try Megan and Cara too, later on in the term." Mrs Ross smiled at her. "You look pleased. I think you'll make a very useful addition to the team. We could do with some more strong forward players."

Mrs Ryan wasn't keen on the girls walking home from school completely on their own, so she came to pick Katie up from football, to be met at the gate by a jubilant, bouncing daughter. Katie was so excited it took a good minute for Mrs Ryan to work out what she was saying.

"Katie, that's wonderful. Do you know when you'll be playing?" she enthused, as soon as she'd translated Katie's hysterical squeaking.

"Not for a couple of weeks. Oh, Mum, it's so unfair, if only Dad was coming a couple of weeks later, he could have seen me play."

Mrs Ryan sighed. "I know. But I'm sure he will be able to one of these days. We'll send him photos of you, sweetie."

Meanwhile Becky and Annabel were in their bedroom, Becky stretched out on her bed reading a cat magazine, lusting after a gorgeous spotty Bengal cat that looked a bit like a baby leopard, and Annabel curled into a most uncomfortable-looking position on the floor, drawing. She knew she ought to be learning her French, but twenty minutes solid had been as much as she could cope with in one go. Becky had promised to test her later. For the moment she was relaxing, although in a slightly depressing way. Her big A3 pad was covered in delicate, detailed little drawings – designs for birthday parties. Annabel loved art, and combining it with clothes and parties was even better. She sat up and stretched – her bottom had gone to sleep – and looked sadly down at her page. This party was magic-themed. It had quite a lot of the glitteriness from her and Saima's original idea, but with added cool costume bits – sparkly wings, pretty gauzy dresses. Annabel gazed at it critically. Cute, but a bit seven-year-old. She supposed that she and Becky and Katie were too old for dressing up . . . but the costumes were still fun to draw. Annabel looked over at Becky, engrossed in her magazine, kicking her feet rhythmically back and forth as she read, one hand creeping perilously close to her mouth as she gradually forgot she'd given up sucking her thumb. Maybe not. Becky looked up. "What're you drawing, Bel?"

Annabel made a face. "Parties," she sighed. "*Imaginary* parties, seeing as we're not getting the real thing."

Becky shut her magazine and wriggled closer to the end of the bed so she could hang over the edge and talk to Bel on the floor. She put out a hand and hooked the pad round. "Oh, sweet!" she exclaimed, laughing at the sparkly designs Annabel had created. The fairy costumes twinkled – Annabel had been using her favourite metallic pens to add the final touches. "Do you think Mum might change her mind?" Becky asked hopefully, seeing herself in a pair of green and gold wings.

"I don't know – she didn't seem cross with us when we got home, did she? Perhaps we should talk to her about it. Let's ask Katie what she reckons when she gets in from football. Actually, that sounds like them now," she added, jumping up and darting to the window.

It was, and two minutes later Katie was rushing up the stairs to tell them her news.

"Imgoingtobeonthefootballteam!" she yelped. "MrsRossisgoingtoletmeplayinagameafterhalf-term!" She was just as incoherent as she had been with Mum, but Becky and Annabel had no trouble understanding. Quite a lot of the time they didn't really need to finish their sentences – it was something they did more for other people's benefit than their own.

Becky and Annabel hugged her excitedly, just as pleased as she wanted them to be. Katie heaved a sigh of pure satisfaction, and noticed Annabel's drawing pad. "What are those, Bel?"

"Oh, I was so depressed about our party

being off that I couldn't concentrate on anything else. Especially French. They're party designs. That one's for a magical party, and there's some others underneath."

"These are really cute," said Katie, picking up the pad for a closer look. "Awww, Becky look! She's got Pixie in this one!"

"I missed that! Where?" Becky bounced over immediately. "Oh, with little wings tied on her. That's gorgeous. Will you draw it bigger for me, Bel? I want it on the pinboard." The triplets had a huge cork board on one wall of their room for drawings and stuff.

"OK, if you really like it." Annabel flushed, pleased. Sometimes she felt like Becky and Katie thought her drawing was a bit silly. "I put her in because of the name, Pixie – magic, you see? I can't imagine it working, though. We'd be dripping blood if we so much as waved a pair of wings at her."

"Mmm," agreed Katie, remembering what she'd got the last time she'd attempted to give

Pixie a friendly cuddle when the little black cat wasn't in the mood – three deep scratches down her arm as Pixie raked her claws over it. She flicked back through the pages – a slightly mad-looking space-themed party with a cake like the moon rocket from the *Tintin* books, and lots of planets hanging from the ceiling; an *Arabian Nights-looking* design, with everyone in silky harem pants and veils; and – "Ooh, Bel, this is nice!" said Katie.

"Which one? Oh, yeah, the winter one. Just a silly idea, really – I mean we're hardly going to flood the back garden and freeze it so we can ice-skate, are we?" But as Annabel watched Katie showing Becky the glittering icicle decorations and the snowflake invitations she'd designed, and the gorgeous scene of skaters on a snowy lake, she suddenly had her second Brilliant Idea. . .

Mum called them down to help make the tea just then – sausages and mash – and in all the chatter over the meal Becky and Katie didn't notice that Annabel was a bit distracted. When they'd done the washing up, they dragged her off to her homework spot on the stairs, and proceeded to teach her French vocab until it was practically coming out of her *oreilles*. When she was getting almost every word right they called it a day and went off to do the rest of their homework. Katie and Becky both did theirs in their room – it had originally been two bedrooms, but Mr and Mrs Ryan had converted it into one big room for the girls. Now they had space for a big desk for homework. Annabel stayed on the stairs, racing through her English comprehension questions, and the write-up of their science practical, so that she could do some serious thinking. Then she took Mr Hatton's detention slip out of her rucksack, made a disgusted face at it, and went downstairs to talk to Mum.

Mrs Ryan was mostly in the fridge when

Annabel got to the kitchen, and as she only had socks on her feet she managed to get right next to her mother without her noticing. "What are you looking for?" she asked interestedly.

Mrs Ryan jumped, and hit her head – she narrowly escaped decapitating herself on the freezer cabinet. "Ooww! Bel! That really hurt – how did you manage to creep up on me like that?" she said, backing out.

"I didn't!" replied Annabel indignantly. "You were just so much in the fridge you didn't notice. Did you want a yoghurt?" Mrs Ryan was addicted to Mr Men chocolate yoghurts. "They're in the door – look, you put them in there to make them easier to get at."

"Oh yes. Thanks, Bel." Annabel handed her mother a yoghurt, and Mrs Ryan grabbed a teaspoon from the dresser. Annabel beamed at her. This was excellent timing. In the middle of a chocolate yoghurt was absolutely the best time to ask Mum *anything*.

"Spoonful?" Her mother waved the teaspoon at her. Annabel sat down opposite her mother and leant over the table to lick the spoon.

"Mmm. Nice. Mummy, can I talk to you about something?"

"You can't have any more pocket money till next week."

"I didn't want any, why did you think—"

"Sweetness, you only call me Mummy when you're after something. OK, if it's not more pocket money, what have you done? Have you broken something upstairs?"

Annabel sighed. The triplets tended to think of their mother as a bit scatty – Annabel had inherited the scattiness, but somehow, it had come out tripled in her. Mum had an annoying habit of being really on the ball just when they least expected it, though.

"I haven't broken anything. But I did get into trouble at school." She was looking at the table as she said this, and now she flicked a quick glance across at her mum. How was she going to take this?

Mrs Ryan put the yoghurt down. Bad sign – she obviously didn't want to be distracted by it. "Hmmm?"

"I did really badly in my French test." Annabel paused, and then gabbled the rest. "I only got six out of forty and Mr Hatton put me in detention."

"*Six?*" squeaked her mother in horror. "How did you manage to only get *six*? You don't find French that hard, do you?"

"No, of course not," said Annabel disgustedly. "I forgot to learn it, that's all."

"Oh, that's all. Really, Bel, I suppose this was what you were supposed to be doing the night you and Katie had that argument," said Mrs Ryan crossly. "Well I have to say, I think you deserve to be in detention."

Hmmm. This was not going well.

"Oh, well, I suppose at least you're honest enough to tell me about it," sighed Mrs Ryan, picking up the yoghurt again, but staring into the pot as if something horrible had drowned in it.

Annabel summoned up her best smile. "Mmm. You have to sign the detention slip. . ."

Having got that out of the way, Annabel decided it would be best to leave the yoghurt to work its magic for a couple of minutes before she got to work on the more important part of her mission:

"Mum, you know on Tuesday you said we couldn't have a party. . ."

Chapter Eight

Annabel had come back upstairs that night looking fairly smug, but Katie and Becky put it down to her not having got into trouble with Mum about her French – Bel was lucky that way. She avoided having to talk too much to her sisters by grabbing her French vocab book and curling up in bed with it, saying she needed to do some serious learning – after all, they could hardly argue with that.

The next morning, though, there was no avoiding the subject of parties. The French disaster and its aftermath, followed by Katie's exciting news, had nearly driven Mum's birthday party ban out of Becky's and Katie's minds. But as soon as they got up on Thursday morning, Becky remembered.

"Katie, Mum's in a good mood at the moment, isn't she? With your being in the football team? Do you think if we asked her ever so nicely, and promised her we wouldn't fight about it, we could convince her to let us have a party?"

"Maybe," conceded Katie cautiously. "She *was* really pleased about the football. It might be worth a try. What do you reckon, Bel?"

Annabel, who'd been brushing her hair and grinning to herself in the mirror, realized that she ought to be taking more of an interest here, or the others would really start to suspect. "Mmm. I think so. Let's try." She couldn't hide a smug, excited sort of smile, but luckily the others just thought she was keen on the idea.

The triplets were particularly polite at breakfast, handing each other things without being asked, and smiling a lot, as if to say that the idea of them fighting about a party was absurd – they were devoted sisters. Of course, they *were,* but today they were making sure that everybody knew it.

After a while of extra-quiet, extra-polite toast-munching, punctuated by milk-slurping from Annabel who was having cereal, Katie caught Becky's eye and waggled her eyebrows in a way that made her look positively demonic. They had decided earlier that as Becky hadn't actually been part of the argument that had got Mum so angry, she had better be the one to bring the subject up again.

"Mum?" wavered Becky, while Katie nodded encouragingly at her.

"Mmmm?" said her mother through a mouthful of toast.

"We were wondering. . ." Katie rolled her eyes in disgust and made a "Get on with it!" face. "Well, we were wondering about what you said about our birthday party? That we couldn't have one because we were fighting? We're really, really sorry and everything, and we thought maybe, if we come up with something that we'd all like, could we still have a party? If we were brilliantly good?"

All three of the triplets fixed their eyes on their mother anxiously. Annabel was faking the anxious look, but she was very convincing. She couldn't resist quickly dropping one eyelid in a wink at her mother, though, when she was certain the other two weren't looking.

Mrs Ryan looked thoughtfully up at the ceiling, and then at her toast, enjoying teasing Katie and Becky. Then, "As it happens," she said slowly, "I was thinking about that myself." She got up and went over to the dresser, picking up a big brown envelope. Then she tipped the contents on to the table – a cascade of sparkly, silvery cards.

The triplets stared at them in amazement. Then Katie said, "Can we touch. . .?"

"Of course, darling. Read one," answered Mrs Ryan, smiling hugely.

Katie gingerly picked up one of the cards,

and her sisters leant over to look at it with her. On the front was a snowflake, cut out of shining, pearly paper that caught the light in loads of different colours somehow. She opened it up and read out, "'Please come to our party! Annabel, Becky and Katie would love you to come and celebrate their birthday' – Mum, this is brilliant! You changed your mind?"

"What sort of party is it, though?" asked Becky, sounding confused, but excited. "Oh, and when is it? Is it that same Saturday, the day after Dad comes?"

Katie checked the date. "Yes, from 2 p.m. until 8 p.m. Wow, that's ages. What are we going to do, Mum? We were going to ask you if we could try and work out something we'd all like, have a sleepover, maybe, but we hadn't thought of anything much yet."

Mrs Ryan gave them a smile that looked scarily like Annabel at her very smuggest. "I'm not telling you, I'm afraid. You'll find out on the day – it's a surprise. Now, there are ten invitations there – all you have to do is give them out, and tell whoever you're giving them to to get their parents to phone me and tell me if they can come. Then I can give them their instructions." Another deeply smug smile.

"Their instructions?" echoed Katie, intrigued. "Mum, what are you planning? This sounds so cool!"

Mrs Ryan just looked down at her watch. "You need to get going, girls, or you'll be late. Don't forget the invitations, will you? We haven't got a lot of time left before the party."

There was no danger of that. Katie swept them up and back into the envelope, and then bore it reverently out to the hall to put it in her rucksack. Becky followed her, and Annabel loitered at the kitchen door until she was sure they were out of earshot.

"Mum, you're a star! Those invites look gorgeous – how did you do them so quickly? Katie and Becky loved them!"

"Well, let's just say I'm going to fall asleep on the sofa this afternoon. It was just lucky I had the paper and the glitter, that's all. Annabel darling, do you really think you'll be able to keep all your plans a secret from Katie and Becky? You know keeping quiet isn't your strong point! Wouldn't it be easier to tell them?"

Annabel looked very determined, and set her mouth in a firm line, frowning at her mother. "I am *not* telling them! Sorry, Mum – I didn't mean to snap, but I *really* don't want to tell them. They laughed at me when I tried to keep my idea of the party a secret the first time, it was *so* annoying. They didn't mean it that way, but it was like, *Oh, poor Bel's so ditzy, she can never keep secrets* – well, I'm going to show them now. This is going to be the best birthday they've ever had, and I'm going to organize it perfectly, and it's got to be a complete surprise. You *mustn't* tell them, Mum!"

Mrs Ryan was surprised. Annabel never being able to keep secrets – even down to what was for pudding or what she was going to wear the next day – was a family joke, she just had this *need* to tell people about things. Her mother hadn't realized that it upset her. She'd been noticing over the past few weeks that now they were at secondary school the triplets really seemed to be growing up and changing – amazingly fast. "Don't worry," she soothed. "I won't. It's a lovely plan, Bel. I'm very proud of you, you know."

"Come on, Bel!" came the screech from the hall. "What are you *doing*?"

Annabel dashed over and gave her mother a hug. "See you later! Thanks again, Mum!"

The triplets raced off to school, desperate to tell their friends that the birthday party of the year was back on. Halfway there, Annabel suddenly stopped dead. "Hang on! We haven't worked out who we're giving these invitations to yet. We ought to do that before we get to school – we can't exactly go back to someone and say sorry, we've changed our minds."

"*You* could, Bel – no one would be surprised," laughed Katie.

"Ha, ha and again, let me see, *ha*," said Annabel, thinking back a little irritably to what she'd just been saying to Mum. "Be serious. Who are we going to invite?"

"Hmm. Ten invitations. Well, Megan and Fran and Saima for a start."

"And Fiona? I know we don't see as much of her as we used to now we're all at Manor Hill, but she's really sweet," suggested Becky.

"Yes, definitely Fiona," agreed Katie.

"There's one really important thing we need to decide," mused Annabel, still in serious mode. "Are we going to invite any boys? I mean, lots of our friends are boys, but do we want them at our party?"

Katie made a face, scrunching up her nose.

"It's difficult – we don't know what we're going to be *doing*, so how do we know if it'll be weird having boys there."

"I think we should have boys," broke in Becky firmly. "I don't think Mum would have organized anything really girly, or she'd have told us to stick to inviting girls. I mean, she knows there are boys we hang around with sometimes."

Annabel carefully didn't let her relieved expression show. She'd been desperately trying to think of a way to convince the others that it would be OK to invite boys without showing that she was in on the secret.

"OK," agreed Katie. "So, we've still got six more invites! Did you want to ask Jack and Robin, Becky?"

"Oooh," giggled Annabel. "Very keen, Katie! Something you're not telling us? Which one, hmm?"

"Shut up, Bel," snapped her sister, embarrassed. "Just because you can't think of anything except boys and make-up, it doesn't mean I can't."

Annabel sniggered. "Can we invite Jordan and Matthew? They're fun, they'd be good to have at a party. Just two left now?"

"Mmm. I think we should ask Moira, you know, she lives near Saima? She's nice. It's hard to know who to give the last invitation to, though – I mean, there's lots of people I like in our class, but I'm not sure I like *one* of them more than anyone else." Katie nibbled her thumbnail in a distracted way.

"Well, I think we should ask David Morley," said Becky, a bit hesitantly.

Annabel and Katie looked blank.

"You know! That boy who has to sit with Amy and Emily and Cara in history. The poor boy never, ever speaks to them, and they just pretend he's not there. I feel sorry for him, he still hardly knows anyone, and he had to move away from all his old friends. I reckon he *needs* a party invitation more than anyone else."

Katie and Annabel exchanged glances, and decided that Becky was being soft-hearted and Becky-ish, and thinking of David as a kind of cross between a boy and a stray dog. It was probably best to humour her.

"And besides," Becky added unexpectedly. "You should look at him, Bel. He's cute, under all that hair. Honestly. A bit like an Old English Sheepdog."

Annabel sighed. Great – now a boy/Old English Sheepdog cross was coming to her perfect party. . .

Chapter Nine

The triplets delivered all the gorgeous invitations that morning, feeling remarkably smug, and making sure that everyone saw that their party was very much on again. Saima, Megan and Fran were suitably excited, and desperate to know what kind of party it was going to be.

"We can't tell you!" Katie laughed. "We honestly don't know! But Mum is *really* good at parties," she assured them. "I mean, just look at the invitations. She's excellent at that kind of stuff. I'm so excited, and it's only nine days away!"

"You can all come, can't you?" asked Annabel anxiously.

"Definitely," said Saima, and Fran and Megan seemed pretty certain too. Fiona, Moira, Matthew, Jordan, Jack and Robin got their invites at registration, under the disgusted eyes of Amy and co. Max made some nasty comments about the boys going to a *"girls'* party" (said in an incredibly disdainful voice). But Matthew and Jordan, who sat quite close to him and his mate Ben, just gave them the kind of look one gives a two-year-old sister who's just been sick over one's DS3 (Matthew's sister had done this twice, so he had it down to a fine art) and Max shut up.

The class was still waiting for Miss Fraser to arrive to take the register, so Becky nipped up to the front table where David Morley was sitting with a couple of other boys, vaguely looking at his science practical write-up, as though he thought he might have remembered it all wrong. Becky was within half a metre of him when she realized that Katie and Annabel weren't following her as she'd thought. She cast an outraged, panicky look over her shoulder – they were still chatting to Matthew and Jordan and enjoying ignoring Max. Well, she couldn't just turn round and go back, that would look really silly. She took a deep breath and faltered, "David?"

David looked up – one of the pretty, popular Ryan triplets was standing next to him looking distinctly nervous.

"Hello," said the nervous triplet – he hadn't a clue which one it was, but he muttered, "Hello, er. . ." which seemed to do.

"Um, hello," said Becky again, and then pulled herself together. "We wondered – me and my sisters, that is – if you'd like to come to our birthday party. It's in half-term. Our phone number's on the invitation – can you get your mum or dad to phone my mum about the details? Thanks!" And then she bolted back to her seat, leaving David looking like a cross between a boy and an Old English

Sheepdog and a tomato, and feeling just as mixed-up.

The triplets had never been more desperate for a school holiday to arrive. Their dad would be staying in the tiny flat he had not far from their house, which he used when he was back in England. Annabel had had a very good go at getting Mrs Ryan to let them take the last Friday off school so they could all go and meet him at the airport, but her mother wasn't having it. By the day, though, they were all in such a state of jittery anticipation that it probably wouldn't have made much difference if they *had* taken the day off. Interesting-looking things kept appearing in the kitchen cupboards, and their mother was wandering around the house looking busy and panicky – and then decidedly furtive as soon as she caught sight of Katie or Becky. Her bedroom had become a Forbidden Zone. Annabel was finding the secret-keeping very difficult but she was still totally determined. What made it all so much harder was that she couldn't let on that she had a secret at all, and she had to keep pretending to Becky and Katie that she was just as bemused and desperate to know what was going on as they were. Dad was in on the secret, obviously, as he was going to be helping organize the party, and he'd sent a series of tantalizing emails, which seemed to have the words "party" and "presents" in every sentence.

Mrs Ryan and Annabel were finding it almost impossible to snatch time to discuss the party without Becky or Katie popping up unexpectedly to ask what they were whispering about. The longest time they'd had to work stuff out was the walk home from school the Friday before, when Mum had gone to fetch Annabel after her detention. Annabel had been fairly confident about her second French test – after all, Becky and Katie had spent the previous evening snapping their fingers in her face in a particularly annoying way and then yelling French words to demand an immediate translation. Most of their vocab list felt as though it was carved into her brain. Mr Hatton was very impressed with her thirty-eight out of forty, and spent ages telling her that if only she'd put the effort in in the first place she could be really good at French, waffle, waffle, while Annabel nodded vigorously and attempted to look suitably sorry. Then she'd dashed out of school to meet Mum and banish French from her head entirely by planning how to decorate the house for the party. Annabel was still in favour of repainting the living room glittery. She'd reminded Mum about it every day that week, in very subtle ways like leaving her glitter nail polish lying round, but Mrs Ryan was holding out. Annabel felt that she and Mum were well on track, though. Annabel did a lot of drawing and painting anyway, so provided she was careful she could make party decorations without the other two realizing what she was doing. Mum had a cake-decorating book, and another one with good ideas for party food, so Annabel had spent quite a lot of time in the evenings hiding in the bathroom making lists, and designing birthday cakes. Katie and Becky thought she was putting intensive conditioner on her hair even more obsessively than usual, in preparation for the party. The week did seem to fly by, though, and Mum had to calm Annabel down when she had a mild panicking session on Thursday night as she was convinced they'd never get it all done.

The next day, scarily enough, was actually the day before the party, and the triplets were mentally ticking off the minutes of their last lesson of the afternoon. How could geography go on so long? Was it some kind of time warp? Mrs Travers let them start packing up five minutes early – even she could see that the last few minutes before half–term were not the best time to introduce Year Seven to the mysteries of sedimentary rocks.

"See you tomorrow!" the triplets yelled to Megan as they set off home with Saima and Fran, who had been warned that if they wanted to walk with them they had to go *fast*. It was probably the first time they'd gone down the high street without stopping to look at any of the shops – without stopping at all, in fact.

The triplets practically broke the front door down, jumping up and down in frustration as Katie fiddled with the key, and then hurling themselves into the hall. Yes! Bags and parcels that definitely hadn't been there this morning.

"Dad!" squawked Katie rapturously, rushing headlong into the kitchen and screeching to a stop next to the table – there he was, banging down his coffee mug to leap up and seize them all in a massive hug.

"Watch it, you three," Mum warned, laughing, "your dad's not going to be much use at your party if you strangle him now."

They disengaged themselves reluctantly, and Dad sat down again. Becky and Katie, almost unable to let go of him, even for a second, leant themselves up against his chair, and Annabel perched herself on the table.

Mr Ryan shook his head, looking around at them. "How long is it since I've seen you? Three months, is that all? You look so different. . ." he tailed off, and then appealed to his ex-wife. "I'm not imagining it, am I? They've grown?"

Mrs Ryan nodded. "Oh yes. They never stop."

"And you've never seen us in our Manor Hill uniform either, Dad – that's different," Annabel broke in.

"True. You look very smart, Bel. Very sensible and businesslike – we get the full party girl outfit tomorrow, do we?"

"*Oh* yes. And I'm going to make up Becky and Katie, and do their hair."

"Do you *have* to?" Katie moaned. "You take so long. And I can never tell the difference, anyway."

"This is a party, Katie. You are *going* to look nice, however long it takes. You *promised*." Katie had, in a weak moment the evening before. Annabel had refused to fetch her a reviving chocolate biscuit when she'd been flaked out on the sofa after just managing to break her keepy-uppy record – now at 102. Annabel had cruelly waved the packet round the living-room door until Katie had promised.

"Dad, what are all those things in the hall?" asked Becky, and the other two stopped their half-hearted bickering and pricked up their ears. "I mean, your clothes and things are at the flat, aren't they?"

"Those parcels, sweetheart, are yet another thing you're not allowed to know about." He exchanged a knowing glance with their mum.

The contents of the parcels was secret even to Annabel, who looked very slightly huffy. "Until tomorrow. Oooh, less than twenty-four hours now. Be patient." He smirked a little.

"You are *so* enjoying this," Katie grumbled. "When do we actually get to find out what's going on, Mum? I mean, if you've got to do stuff to the house we're going to see, aren't we?"

"No hints," said their mum firmly. "Not a word, so don't pester, Katie."

And with that the triplets had to be satisfied until the next day.

Chapter Ten

The triplets were up early the next morning. Earlier than Mum, who they woke up mercilessly by calling outside her bedroom door (they still weren't allowed in). Mum had warned them not to even think of getting up before seven, or they'd be exhausted by the end of the party. She'd also pointed out there was no reason to get up early, as nothing was happening till the afternoon. She knew it wasn't going to have much effect, though. And she was right – dead on seven o'clock, they were out of their bedroom, bouncing and yelping excitedly to get her up and get the day properly started. They'd spent at least the last half hour awake and chatting curled up on

Annabel's bed, and she was beginning to be really glad the pretence wouldn't have to go on much longer. Katie had already accused her of not really being excited about the party as she wasn't saying enough. Annabel had claimed she was just sleepy, and the other two seemed to believe her — after all, she *did* like to sleep in at the weekends.

Mrs Ryan appeared in her dressing gown. "What time is it, for heaven's sake? Two minutes past seven — I might have known. Well, as you're so energetic you can go and put the kettle on and make me some coffee and toast while I have a shower."

The triplets raced downstairs as Mum shuffled into the bathroom, but stopped halfway as she called after them, "Don't forget! You *can't* go in the living room!" Ten minutes later she appeared in jeans and a jumper looking considerably more awake, and once she'd got a cup of coffee in her hands she was almost human.

"Mum, please will you tell us what's going on today now?" begged Katie, blue eyes like saucers.

"Pleease!" asked Becky beseechingly.

"Your dad and I will tell you at lunchtime. I've got loads to do before then, so get lost please. I need you upstairs and out of the way."

"You mean we can't be in the kitchen, *either*?" demanded Katie in horror.

"Not unless you're going to sit blindfolded with a clothes-peg on your nose. Go on upstairs – have baths, wash your hair. Let Annabel do your nails, that should take a good three hours."

Annabel stuck her tongue out at her mother, but said, "Actually, that's a really good idea, I hadn't thought about nails. C'mon, Katie."

"We said make-up," squeaked Katie in outrage. "Nothing about nails!"

"Do you have anything else to do this morning?"

"Nooo, but. . ."

Annabel grabbed her and marched her upstairs, still muttering.

By midday the triplets were cleaner and more beautified than they had ever been. Even Katie had had intensive hair conditioner (they'd used an entire new tub between them – they had a lot of hair), a face pack and a manicure that had left her squirming with impatience at having to sit still for so long and Annabel wondering whether she really wanted to give her sisters a party at all. Katie was stomping about their bedroom like a really wild wildebeest, casting disgusted glances at her perfect "Ice Queen" pale blue nails. She had utterly refused to let Annabel put a small crystal on the tip of each one, in fact she'd threatened to go and clean the whole lot off if Annabel so much as brought a nail jewel within half a metre of her hands.

The triplets were still in everyday clothes – jeans and sweaters. They didn't know (or, in

Annabel's case, had to *pretend* not to know) what sort of clothes they needed for the party, so Becky and Annabel had laid out a selection on their beds (and Annabel had laid out Katie's too) and were squabbling pleasantly about who ought to wear what. Annabel's scarlet pleated miniskirt was going head to head with Becky's slightly different and horribly clashing scarlet fluffy sweater when there was a knock at the bedroom door.

"Everyone decent?" called Dad, and Katie raced to open the door. "Can we come downstairs?" she burst out. "I have to get out of here. Those two are driving me mad!"

Dad grinned. "Go and run up and down the garden till you feel better, sweetheart. Come on, you two," he added as Katie shot past him and thundered down the stairs, "Mum sent me to fetch you for lunch."

"When did you get here, Dad?" asked Becky, puzzled. "We didn't hear you arrive."

"I came in the back gate. I needed to help

your mum set things up and she reckoned you'd be fussing even more if you knew I was here too."

The kitchen was spotless, with no evidence of party preparation at all. The triplets looked round suspiciously. "Are you sure you've been doing anything this morning, Mum?" asked Katie.

"It's all hidden away. Right, lunch. Treat food, as today is temporarily your birthday."

"Nachos, excellent," cheered Annabel, as Mum brought a mound of tortilla chips, salsa and gorgeous, oozing melted cheese to the table. "Katie Ryan, if you damage those nails I will personally cut your fingers off, got it?"

"You see, this is why I don't wear nail polish," Katie moaned. "You can't do *anything*. What am I supposed to do, pick up nachos with my teeth?"

"Just be careful. It's supposed to be chip-resistant, but then it's never met *you* before."

Annabel daintily picked up a nacho, managing not even to get a smudge of grease on her sparkly silver nails.

Dad let them all get well stuck into the nachos and then raised his eyebrows at Mum. "What do you think? Time to spill the beans?"

Becky choked with excitement and had to be thumped on the back, slightly over-enthusiastically as Katie was desperate to know what was going on.

Mum smiled. "Annabel?"

"What are you asking Bel for?" Katie sounded confused. "We *all* want to know."

"I'm asking Bel because this was all her idea," said Mum, leaving Katie opening and shutting her mouth like a very gormless goldfish. "Annabel came up with the theme for a party that all three of you would like, and she's kept it secret from you two all this time."

"So it's not a surprise party for Bel at all?" asked Becky, looking from Mum to Annabel and back again. "You've been pretending all this time?"

"Are you cross?" asked Annabel.

"No, I'm just really, really amazed – that you managed not to say anything, all those conversations we had about what it was going to be, and you *knew*!" She sounded quite sorry for Annabel, as she added, "And you're not even getting a surprise party!"

"No, but I get to see you and Katie having it – I'm terrified you won't like it though. And I haven't seen the decorations or the food or anything so that's all a surprise. . ." Annabel faltered to a stop. Katie still hadn't said anything. Was she furious? Did she think Annabel had taken over and organized everything her own way, like she had complained about before? There was no way to tell – Katie's face wasn't giving anything away. Annabel carried on. "Katie, do you remember that drawing I did, of the ice-skating party? The one you really liked? I was trying to think

127

of something that I'd love to do for our birthday, but that you and Becky would like, too. And I thought, *ice-skating*. I mean, it's kind of girly and fun but sporty at the same time. I know that doesn't really have anything specially for you, Becky, but—"

"But I'd *love* to go ice-skating!" Becky interrupted. "That's what we're doing? That's so cool! Isn't it, Katie?" she demanded, kicking her sister under the table. Annabel looked so worried that Becky would probably have said, "Yay!" to extra French if that had been the party plan, but she really did love the idea.

Katie swallowed. She had to admit, ice-skating did sound brilliant, and Annabel had made a real effort to make them all happy – but this was Bel! Her dippy sister who spent her life thinking about make-up and clothes and boys and *never* organized anything, least of all herself. It was almost impossible for Katie to believe that Annabel had done all this while she and Becky had just sat around, so in the dark that they were practically asleep. But she had. "It'll be fab, Bel," she said, getting up and going to give her a hug. "Thanks. You're a star."

"Anyone want to know what's in those parcels in the hall?" asked Dad in an offhand kind of way.

"Yees," squeaked the triplets, the difficult moment temporarily forgotten.

"Shall I get them?" asked Katie, who was still on her feet.

"Uh-huh." Dad was looking very smug.

"Do you know what these are, Bel?" asked Katie, as she came back with her arms full of silvery wrapping paper, a slight edge to her voice.

"Not a clue, honestly," Annabel promised her, and Katie relaxed. She didn't think she could stand her sister knowing *everything*.

The remains of the nachos were cleared away, and the fabulous parcels laid out on the table. Sparkling paper, metres and metres of fat satiny ribbon in gorgeous colours – the triplets couldn't wait to rip them apart. . .

"Oh wow!" murmured Annabel, who'd somehow managed to untie the ribbon without tying herself in knots like the other two. "Look!" She held up a blue satin skirt, trimmed with fluffy feathers. "It's perfect, it's like the ones I drew – oh, Dad, you are so clever! Come on, you two, I want to see what yours are!"

By this time, Becky had got into her parcel to find a pale pink cardigan with silvery fake-fur at the collar and cuffs, and Katie was just giving up on the untying option and tearing the paper off her present – purple cord jeans, cute but still very Katie.

"OK to wear for skating?" asked Dad anxiously. "I wanted party-ish clothes that you wouldn't freeze in, so I made a detour to Oxford Street on my way home yesterday. Your mum did the wrapping, though. Not sure why we bothered. . ." he added, smiling down at the litter of silver scraps – all that was left of the pretty parcels.

"You'd better go and change," said Mum, checking her watch. "It's only an hour before you need to leave."

"No!" gasped Annabel in horror. "Get upstairs now, we have to do make-up and don't you dare try and get out of it, Katie."

An hour and a half later the triplets were meeting the rest of the party at the ice rink and heading off to get their skates. They looked amazing. Mum didn't really like them wearing make-up to school (the school didn't either) and Katie and Becky could never be bothered anyway. Annabel normally just made do with clear tinted nail polish and lipgloss which she knew she could get away with. Dad had been speechless when they came back downstairs – and that was after Mum had warned him not to throw a fit. He wasn't sure he liked his little girls looking so grown-up.

Annabel thought she'd been quite restrained – this was only daytime make-up, they'd get the glitter out later on. . .

The triplets' friends were a bit gobsmacked, too. They were used to telling the three of them apart by a relatively simple method – the one with the nail polish and hair full of clips and braids and whatever was Annabel, the sporty-looking one with no-nonsense hair was Katie, and Becky was the one somewhere in between. Now, though, at first glance you had three Annabels with the most amazing blonde curls. Once they thought about it, it was fairly obvious that Katie was the one in trousers, and Annabel was definitely feathery-skirt-girl. David edged up to the triplet struggling with her laces whom he reckoned was Becky. "Um, hello. You look, um, nice. Different. But nice." Then he decided it would be a good idea to shut up.

Becky blushed. She wasn't used to compliments. "Thanks. It's nice that you could come."

"Mmm, I really like ice-skating. There was a rink close to where I lived before."

"I've never done it. I'm not sure I'm going to be able to stand up!"

"I could help you, um, if you like?"

The huge expanse of shiny white ice that they'd seen on the way in had looked so scary and slippery that Becky said yes without even thinking about it. When they got on the ice David turned out to be good enough to skate *backwards*, so he held her hands and towed her round the ring. It was brilliant. Becky thought back to her fantasy birthday party, polar-bear-watching in the arctic. If she half closed her eyes, that could be a polar bear on that patch of ice. . . By the time they'd got right the way round everybody else had fallen over at least three times and the triplets' dad was choking with laughter. He'd flatly refused to come on the ice with them – he said he needed to take photos, and anyway he liked being in one piece, thank you very much. As Becky arrived back, not a hair out of place, the rest of the girls looked hopefully at David, who went deeply red – they were staring at him!

"That was so cool, you're really good at this," whispered Becky. "Would you take all the others, too? I think they could do with some help!"

David gulped and nodded, and Becky let go of him *very* carefully. "Bel, do you want David to show you what to do? It really helps you get your balance – ooh!" She wobbled massively and grabbed the safety rail. "Well, OK, I *was* balancing."

David skated over to Katie, who was clinging on to Fran and Megan for dear life. She grinned at him. "Actually, *that's* Annabel over there, but show me first!"

They set off slowly round the rink, David encouraging her to lean forward. He had a very scientific explanation about centres of gravity, but Katie was concentrating too hard on her toes to really get it.

By the end of the two-hour session, most of the party could just about skate on their own – with the exception of Robin, whose nose seemed to have a fatal attraction to the ice. Katie, of course, had got really good at it after a bit of practice, as she seemed to have natural balance. The boys had been a bit dismissive when they first realized what they were going to do. ("Ice-skating's *girly*," Matthew had said to Jordan in disgust.) But after the first few falls they just got more and more determined to be as good as that David Morley. David was having a much better time than he'd expected. Half the prettiest girls in his class were begging him for help, and it was hard to be shy with someone when they'd nearly fallen on top of him a few times.

Annabel couldn't believe it when she spotted Dad waving and pointing at his watch. "Look!" she said indignantly to Saima. "It's not been two hours, has it?" But it had, and there were Saima's dad and Megan's dad, who'd been roped in to help ferry everybody back to the triplets' house.

Luckily, the car Annabel was in arrived back first, so she just had time to rush upstairs and change into her party outfit. She pulled on her favourite pair of white trousers with a pink belt and her glittery silver top. She dabbed on some extra glitter and hurried downstairs. Annabel had been looking forward to this bit of the party almost more than the skating. She and Mum had worked together on the decorations and a few times she'd been able to get away from Katie and Becky and sneak into Mum's room to see how her bits were going – but she hadn't been able to help put everything up, and she was desperate to see the final effect.

It was worth the wait. The general reaction was "Wow!" as everyone crowded in through the door. The ceiling was entirely covered in swags of silvery net, with sparkling snowflakes hanging from it. The living room was painted blue, so it went together pretty well.

On the table in front of the window was another big, silvery parcel, and the party guests added their own presents – it was a massive pile! "*Another* present from you, Dad?" asked Annabel, confused.

"Nope, this one's from your mum as well. It's for all of you – go on, open it, it should fit into the party nicely, we thought." He grinned at them.

Everyone watched with interest as the triplets attacked the parcel. Was it some kind of party game?

"Excellent! A PlayStation 4!" yelped Jordan, seeing the familiar logo as the triplets ripped off the paper. "What games have you got?" He leant over Saima to peer at the three games on top of the box. "That football one's brilliant! And what's that – a *dance* game?" He couldn't have sounded more horrified.

"Oh no, I think you need a special mat-thingy for that," Saima put in worriedly, but the triplets' dad was waving another box.

"Special added extra for Annabel, for thinking up the whole party idea. And this one here's for you, Becky. Lots of cute furry animals in it, apparently."

Jack exchanged glances with the other boys, and "coughed". "Uh – *babyish*!"

Annabel poked him in the side. "Yeah?" she whispered. "Just because you don't know how to play it." Then she said loudly, "Bet Becky could beat you at it any day!"

Becky gave her a slightly dismayed look.

"OK," suggested Robin. "Tournament. Boys v Girls. You up for it?" He looked round at everyone else – definitely yes.

"There's more girls, though," said David.

"Yeah, but they're *girls*. C'mon, no problem. And Mr Ryan'll play for us. Won't you?" he asked the triplets' dad, who was halfway behind the television trying to connect up all the leads for the PlayStation. "You need this one, in there," said Robin, dangling it in front of him.

"Oh, right. There, is it working?"

"Yes," called Annabel, grabbing one of the controllers. "Right. You're going to be so sorry, Robin."

An hour later the sofa and armchairs were two deep in people screaming encouragement as Annabel and her dad battled it out.

"Yes!" Annabel cheered as her character did a little victory dance on the screen. "How many games ahead are we, Robin?" she asked sweetly.

He muttered something.

"Sorry, didn't hear you. Three, was that? Would you like to give up now, or shall we come back and beat you up some more after tea?"

"We're only letting them win 'cause it's their birthday," Jack growled to the other boys as they headed for the kitchen, and Annabel rolled her eyes at Becky and Katie. *So* not true.

She looked round the kitchen — more snowflakes on the walls, the table loaded with food. Things were definitely good. Dad was home — if only for a week. Katie and Becky were ooohing at the gorgeous white chocolate birthday cake that Mum had made following Bel's design — in fact, everyone seemed to be having the best time, even if the boys were now making frantic plans to destroy the girls at Katie's football game.

"Come on, Bel!" Katie called. "We need you to blow the candles out!"

"Thought about your wish, Bel?" Dad asked her, smiling.

Annabel stood between Becky and Katie, getting ready to blow out the thirty-three candles, and thought that maybe her birthday wish had already come true. . .

Read the opening of the
next Triplets book:

Katie's
Big
Match

Chapter One

"Come on, come on, come on — yeeeeeessssss!" Becky and Mum leaped up and down and cheered as Manor Hill scored another goal. Or to be precise, *Katie* scored another goal. It was Katie's first game for the team, and Mrs Ross, the junior team coach, was looking extremely smug. Putting Katie Ryan up front had definitely been a good idea.

Annabel was decidedly less enthusiastic about the whole thing. "So that was good then, was it?" she muttered gloomily.

Becky and Mum glared at her.

"Annabel!" said Becky disgustedly. "You know perfectly well that was a goal — Katie's *second* goal. You're just being stupid. I mean, I'm not that into football either, but it's so exciting! Katie's brilliant at this! Look, the other team's coach looks as though she could quite happily tear Katie into little bits and jump on them," she concluded bloodthirstily, beaming happily at the seething coach, who actually looked as though Katie's identical triplets were on her tearing and stomping list as well.

"But it's so co-old. . ." moaned Annabel. "And I'm hungry, and my feet hurt. Couldn't we have brought chairs?" she suddenly appealed to Mum.

"Annabel, the sun is shining, it's only October, and you are wearing a jacket, a scarf, a hat and *mittens*, for heaven's sake! And you've only been standing for half an hour," said Mrs Ryan in response.

Annabel surveyed her outfit happily – it was the only thing bearable about this boring afternoon. A mind-numbingly tedious Geography lesson (somehow always worse on a Friday, impossible though that might seem) and now being forced to watch *football*. She stroked the tassels of her cream-and-pink-striped scarf against her cheek, then tugged the matching hat closer round her ears and shivered dramatically for Mum's benefit. Of course, there was no way she'd have missed Katie's first football match, but she was going to make sure that everybody appreciated her being there as much as possible. Especially as she had some serious beginning-of-the-weekend lounging around the house and blatantly not doing her homework to get on with.

Annabel turned her attention back to the muddy pitch, where Katie's best friend Megan was about to face her first real challenge. It was Megan's first game for the Manor Hill team as well, and she'd been a bit nervous. Katie and Megan were in Year Seven, but most of the team was made up of Year Eights – a couple of whom had been lazy about turning up to practice recently, and

Mrs Ross had *very* definite feelings about that. If you missed practices for no good reason, you didn't get to play, even if it was the league quarter-final. But there had been some sulky muttering among the Year Eights: how come these three Year Seven players had managed to get on to the team in their first year at Manor Hill?

The third new Year Seven player was Cara Peters, which was the only thing taking the shine off it all for Katie. Cara was one of her least favourite people at school – she was one of Amy Mannering's two best friends, and Amy Mannering was the triplets' arch-enemy. Katie couldn't deny that Cara was good, though. In fact, Cara was nearly as good as she was, even though it was torture to admit it. Cara and Katie were both natural strikers, and serious competition for each other. It was just a pity that Cara was a natural pain as well.

Megan was facing her first major challenge

of the game. She was goalie, and up till now most of the action had been up the other end of the pitch as Katie and Cara put on a brilliant display and pretty much dazzled the Hillcrest defence. But now the fierce-looking Hillcrest captain with short, spikey black hair was racing down the field towards Megan with a very grim look on her face. She was seriously fast, and the Manor Hill defence had been resting on its laurels a bit, and been taken by surprise. Now it was the Hillcrest supporters who were holding their breath, and their cross-looking coach had both fists tightly clenched as she watched the black-haired girl getting closer and closer to what would hopefully be their first goal of the match.

Becky, Mum and even Annabel watched anxiously. They liked Megan a lot, and Katie had told them how nervous she was about her first game. It was such a responsibility playing in goal – especially with eight rather hostile twelve year olds just waiting for you to slip up.

Megan didn't *look* worried, though. In fact, now that she had something to do she looked eager, and determined – just as determined as the Hillcrest girl, who was about to take her shot.

Katie reckoned that Megan could actually read minds. How else was it that eight times out of ten she knew which way you were going, and had her gloves in just the right place? When they were practising in the park Megan seemed to know where Katie was putting the ball before Katie did. Certainly she looked pretty confident now. The Hillcrest striker took her shot. The ball sailed towards Megan and she dived expertly to the right. A save! Megan hugged the ball as though she never meant to let it go.

"Yaaaay! Go, Megan!" came a particularly loud cheer – it was all three triplets, yelling completely as one. Several of the other supporters looked quite disconcerted. Megan was grinning hugely as she booted the ball back up the field. It hadn't been a very difficult save, but it had looked great! Her dad was beside himself, bouncing around all over the place and chortling, nudging her mum and pointing out how well Megan had done, while Megan's mum patiently agreed with him.

Becky suddenly felt really sorry for Katie. Their dad should be here, too! Two goals in her first game was absolutely fantastic, and there was no way he'd ever really be able to know what it was like, even though Mum had taken loads of photos. She felt quite cross with Dad all of a sudden – why did he have to work so far away? Megan's dad had obviously taken time off work, but their dad wasn't going to be popping back from Egypt to watch Katie, even if Manor Hill went all the way to the final. She wondered if Katie felt the same way.

Neither team scored in the second half, so it was a jubilant Manor Hill side who romped off the field at fulltime. Three-nil! And Hillcrest were a good team. Katie and Megan came over to the sidelines to be congratulated, looking very pleased with themselves. Katie was looking hopeful, too. "Mum, I don't suppose Megan could come back for tea? If that's all right with you too, Mrs Jones?" she added politely.

Mrs Ryan looked distant for a moment, and the triplets waited patiently. It wasn't that Mum was annoyed, she was just trying to remember what they were having for tea and whether there was enough of it. Finally, she smiled. "That would be fine" – she turned to Megan's parents – "if it fits in with your plans? In fact, if you wanted, Megan could stay the night. The girls are all going into town shopping tomorrow, aren't they?"

"Ooooh, yes! Please, Mum, that would be fab!" Megan pleaded.

"Well, if you're sure it's no trouble. What clothes do you want for tomorrow, Meg?" asked Mrs Jones. "We'll nip home and then your dad'll run them across for you." Then she looked Megan and Katie up and down and grinned. "You sure you've got enough hot water, Sue? These two look like they've been playing in a swamp, not a field."

"Might as well be," said Katie disgustedly. "The goals are like soup."

So it was settled – Megan was sleeping over. She and the triplets raced for the car. There was a brief delay while Mrs Ryan covered every centimetre of upholstery that might possibly come into contact with Katie or Megan in newspaper, and then they headed home.

The tea that Mrs Ryan had been trying to remember was pasta with tomato sauce, and there was plenty to go round, including loads of delicious cheese to melt on top. Katie and Megan were too excited to concentrate much on what they were eating, though. They couldn't believe that they'd won their first match! And not only that, it had been the quarter-final.

"This is only Manor Hill's second year in the schools league," Katie explained to the others, stabbing her fork at Mum for emphasis. "Last year we came absolutely *nowhere*, 'cause Mrs Ross had only just started up the team and they were useless, everyone says so. But if we win the next match, we'll be in the *final*!"

"Oh no!" exclaimed Annabel dramatically. "Does that mean I have to go to *another* football match?"

"Will you definitely get to play?" asked Becky anxiously. It would be awful if Katie and Megan got demoted back to subs again.

Katie looked thoughtful. "What do you reckon, Megan?" she asked her friend, who now had a tomatoey ring round her mouth to match her red hair.

"I'm just not sure." Megan sounded frustrated. "Mrs Ross told Caroline and Michelle and Lizzie that they'd be back on the team if they put the effort in, but from what the others were saying, I don't think they're that bothered. Got better things to do, I suppose." Megan shrugged, as though she really couldn't imagine what.

"I don't see how Mrs Ross could stop you playing after today," said Becky stubbornly, sticking up for her triplet. "I mean, two goals! And you pulled off some brilliant saves, Megan," she added, smiling.

"Yeah, they were fab, especially that one that you dived for. And Cara scored as well," Katie pointed out gloomily, "so we're not getting rid of her either. We'll just have to hope that Mrs Ross thinks we're the best thing for the team. And that Cara breaks her leg," she added with a grin. Then she had a sudden thought. "Mum, can I ring Dad's mobile? To tell him about the match? I know it costs loads, but I'll pay for it out of my pocket money. I know we could wait til later and Skype him when he's home but I just want to talk to him now! Please?"

Mum smiled at her. "Dad's waiting for you to call. He emailed this morning to check he had the right day. Don't forget to give the others a chance to talk too, though."

Katie danced over to the counter to get the phone. "You don't mind, do you, Megan?"

Megan shook her head. "Course not."

Katie dialled, and Dad must have had the phone in his hand, because he picked up immediately, and Katie burst into excited chatter. "We won, Dad! I scored two goals, and now we're in the semi-final!" She'd pressed the speakerphone button, so they all heard his reply.

"Fantastic! Well done, sweetheart! I knew you could do it."

Then they went all technical, so the others decided to have second helpings until Katie and her dad had stopped discussing footwork, and they could talk about "normal stuff". It took quite a long time, but at last Katie passed the phone over to Becky and Annabel, who both huddled over it at the same time, and sat back down at the kitchen table.

"More pasta, Katie?"

"Mmmm." Katie took seconds, and proceeded to push the pasta round her plate. Somehow, telling Dad about her triumphant game, and hearing how excited he was, had made her miss him loads – telling him all about it had been brilliant, but she really wished she hadn't needed to. . .

That night, Megan slept on an inflatable mattress in between the triplets' beds. She and Katie were exhausted after the match (and the twenty minutes of mad puffing it had taken to blow up the mattress) but they were pretty hyper as well, so there was quite a bit of hysterical giggling at things that really weren't all that funny, before Megan suddenly shut up mid-sentence, and had obviously fallen asleep. Becky and Annabel were half-snoozing already (there was only so much fantasy football team-picking they could take) so only Katie was left awake.

She was feeling odd. It had been a brilliant day (two goals! She still couldn't believe it!) but something was not right, and she was pretty sure she knew what it was. She loved Megan loads – she was the first really close friend Katie'd had apart from her sisters, but at 4.42 that afternoon she hadn't liked her much. And that was making her feel really really mean. Katie hadn't been able to help it, though. She'd been cheering Megan's fab save and heard Becky and Annabel yelling too. She'd turned to wave at them and there he was – dancing around like he'd won the lottery – Megan's dad. It was so unfair. No, it was worse than unfair, it was wrong. Why was Megan's dad there to go crazy about a stupid save when *her* dad was in *Egypt*? Katie wasn't really a crying person – she reckoned that Becky had got her share of crybabyness as well as her own – but now she could feel a choking lump in her throat that meant she really wanted to cry. Or, preferably, scream. And shout. Lots. And she wouldn't mind kicking something either – Dad maybe.

Katie sniffed, and sighed, and turned over with a huffy thump, snuggling the duvet around her shoulders. She didn't need Dad there for everything. That was stupid. She had Mum, and she had Becky and Annabel, and they were like having something infinitely better than sisters (and worse, sometimes). This afternoon Annabel had watched an entire football match, and she'd only moaned about it every other sentence for the rest of the evening – for Annabel that was serious sisterly devotion. No, Katie would be fine without Dad. She was making a big fuss about nothing. But as she finally drifted off to sleep, all she could see was one amazingly perfect afternoon in the garden, just before her parents split up. She and Dad playing football, very carefully avoiding the rug where Becky and Annabel were sitting playing with the guinea pigs. Or rather, arguing about whether Annabel could give Maisy a furcut so she could actually see. Dad was cheering – the ball had definitely gone between the two rose bushes – Katie had scored a goal. . .

Look out for more

HOLLY WEBB

Triplets

Becky's Terrible Term

HOLLY WEBB

Triplets

Katie's Big Match

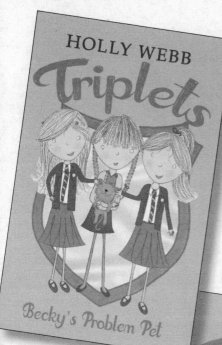

HOLLY WEBB

Triplets

Becky's Problem Pet

HOLLY WEBB

Triplets

Annabel's Starring Role

HOLLY WEBB

Triplets

Katie's Secret Admirer

HOLLY WEBB

Triplets

Becky's Dress Disaster

Look out for

Catmagic
HOLLY WEBB

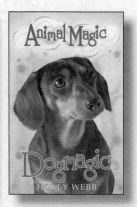

Dogmagic
HOLLY WEBB

Hamstermagic
HOLLY WEBB

Rabbitmagic
HOLLY WEBB

Birdmagic
HOLLY WEBB

Ponymagic
HOLLY WEBB

Mousemagic
HOLLY WEBB

Look out for

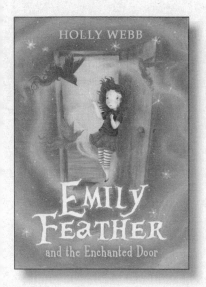

HOLLY WEBB

EMILY FEATHER
and the Enchanted Door

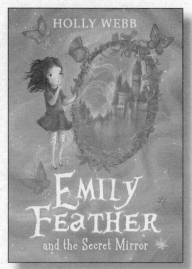

HOLLY WEBB

EMILY FEATHER
and the Secret Mirror

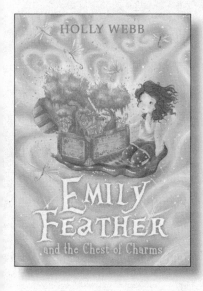

HOLLY WEBB

EMILY FEATHER
and the Chest of Charms

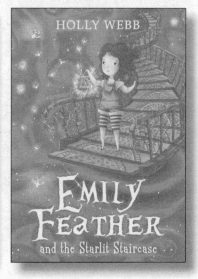

HOLLY WEBB

EMILY FEATHER
and the Starlit Staircase

HOLLY has always loved animals.
As a child, she had two dogs, a cat, and at
one point, nine gerbils (an accident).
Holly's other love is books. Holly now lives
in Reading with her husband, three sons
and a very spoilt cat.

TEN QUICK QUESTIONS FOR HOLLY WEBB

1. Kittens or puppies? Kittens

2. Chocolate or Sweets? Chocolate

3. Salad or chips? Chips

4. Favourite websites? Youtube, Lolcats

5. Text or call? Call

6. Favourite lesson at school? Ancient Greek (you did ask. . .)

7. Worst lesson at school? Physics

8. Favourite colour? Green

9. Favourite film? The Sound of Music

10. City or countryside? Countryside, but with fast trains to the city!